D1613407

LITERATURE AND LANGUAGE DIVISION
THE CHICAGO PUBLIC LIBRARY
400 SOUTH STATE STREET
CHICAGO, ILLINOIS 60605

KILLING WITH THE EDGE OF THE MOON

KILLING WITH THE EDGE OF THE MOON

Copyright © 2005 by A. A. Attanasio

Cover art copyright © 2005 by Timothy Lantz
Interior design © 2005 by Garry Nurrish

Prime Books
www.prime-books.com

Publisher's Note:

No portion of this book may be reproduced by any means, mechanical, electronic, or otherwise, without first obtaining the permission of the copyright holder.

For more information, contact Prime.

Trade HB ISBN: 0-8095-5697-9
Trade PB ISBN: 0-8095-5698-7

KILLING WITH THE EDGE OF THE MOON

A. A. Attanasio

A Graphic Novel
(without illustrations)

PRIME BOOKS

In token of my admiration for a wonderful spirit,
this book is inscribed to you.

RO4O88O1543

Gods, demons, the whole universe, are but a dream,
which exists in the mind, springs from the mind—
and sinks back into the mind.
—Katha Upanishad

CONTENTS

PART ONE
THE MOON IN SILENCE SINGS

Prelude: Dark Ceremony
The Unseen Scene
Woman Made of Flowers
Black Dog
Something Wrong with the Kid
Smacked
The Otherworld
One Crazy Witch
Home Invader
Party Animals
A Bad Place
When You're Here, You're There
Tear It All Down
Zip to Do with Love
Tricked Out Ghost
Cool as in Strange
Wicked Wicca
Pit of Darkness
Maulers' Dance
Deviant
Shining Moment

CONTENTS CONTINUED

PART TWO
KILLING WITH THE EDGE OF THE MOON

Interlude: Walking the Black Dog

Taking Down the Moon

Butt Kick the Crone

There Is a Dragon to Feed

A Classic View of Hell

Jagged Morning

Out of Sight

Evil Strokes

Cold Revelation

Ransack the Pit

Terrors of the Hunt

Killing with the Edge of the Moon

Demented Hope

Love Cut with Fear

What Is What We Cannot Say Is

Breakdown at the Brink

Killing with the Edge of the Moon

Furious Angels

Hellhole

The Fetch

Dreams Pass like Starlight

PART ONE

THE MOON IN SILENCE SINGS

In the days when Mab was queen and the world knew much of magic, dreams were the soul's adventures in the Otherworld. Sometimes the soul got lost or found greater happiness in the Otherworld than in ours, and the sleeper would not wake. Then the sleeper's beloved—if the passion between them was strong enough—undertook a journey beneath the shadow of the moon to the Otherworld and there, by ardor of their love, enticed the soul to return. Such a journey, the old folk called the Fetch.

PRELUDE:
DARK CEREMONY

A witch; and one so strong she could control the moon.
—William Shakespeare, *The Tempest*

Nedra Fell had a face like hickory bark, hair like cobwebs. In the woods at night, beside an altar made from a tree stump, she swayed, and moonlit mist swirled around her thick as smoke.

She mumbled an incantation no more comprehensible than the wind in the branches of the surrounding forest. The flames of two fat black candles on the altar blazed brighter, illuminating stark desperation on her craggy features.

"Obey me!" her entranced voice broke loudly into English. "Obey me, spirits!"

Arthritic hands manipulated crude magical implements upon the altar. She raised a hare-skull goblet. Liquid, thick and dark as blood, glimmered to the brim. Intoning a hoarse salutation to the pocked moon, she sipped the potion. Then, she lowered the small skull between the candles and lifted a hefty wand carved from an elk's thighbone. Its knobby length shook in her trembling grip as she touched it first to a black knife of gleaming volcanic glass then to a broad clamshell filled with loose fangs and yellow incisors.

"Spirits of night extend my days!" She bounced from foot to foot, her gown of coarse hemp jumping as she chanted. "Grant me success in all my ways! Improve my health so my life stays! Seven more years, my death delays! Spirits of night extend my days!"

Jerking like a puppet, Nedra danced about her tree stump altar. Silver threads decorating her long-sleeved gown glittered in the moonlight with embroidered spirals, hex signs and raying stars. Skinny arms, thin as sticks in those wide cuffs, beat the darkness, and long hair jerked across her haggard face.

"Spirits of night, hear my cry! Make me strong so I never die! Spirits of night, hear . . . "

A loud growl from out of the forest froze the old witch, arms stiff above her gray head, hands grasping the elk thighbone more tightly. She stared hard among the trees, where branches sifted moonlight to silver haze.

"I hear you!" she shouted and edged closer to the altar, reaching for the knife of black glass. "I hear you hungering for me. Hungering for my bones. But you can't have me! Not yet, Hela! I've cheated you once again. Oh, yes!"

From out of the moonshadows slid a large dog, thick shoulders shoving forward a faceted head of prodigious evil. The black, muscular beast slouched aggressively into the clearing, ears flat, pale eyes glaring, lips curled back in a fierce grimace.

Nedra Fell gasped. "Too late!" Her warped fingers closed on the black knife. "The chant! The night spirits! You can't have me now, Hela. Try your luck again—in seven years!"

With an explosive bark, the powerful dog lunged. The witch reeled backward and swiped the glass blade before her. Atop the altar, the big mongrel crashed, scattering candles, goblet and fetish bones under splayed claws. Vicious jaws raved. Spittle flew in luminous threads, and barks pummeled the old woman like invisible fists.

The percussive force of the dog's shouts staggered Nedra. "Be gone!" She slashed with the knife and jabbed with the femur big as a club. "You got here late. The spell is cast. You can't have me!"

The bitch attacked, and her slavering teeth seized the cuff of the witch's knife arm. Yanked to the ground by the weight of the mauler, the crone lost her grip on the knife. The blade spun flashing through the moonlight and splashed across the tree stump in tinkling shards.

"No!" The witch shrieked as if her lungs were on fire. "No!" She brought the femur down hard on the ferocious head, and the dog's growling rage split to a damaged yelp. On her belly, the monster scurried backward.

Nedra rolled upright to her knees, eyes bulging with wrath, elk bone raised high. "Devil's cur! Snake spit blind your eyes! You'll not have me!"

The crouching beast watched her with a stare cold as winter windows. The wrinkled snout bared bone-crushing teeth. And she pounced, launching toward the witch in a flurry of black bristles.

Nedra swung the elk bone with all its skull-smashing force. The bitch slid away, elusive as moonlight. She curled about and came in snapping for the old woman's hamstrings. Lurching aside, the crone backhanded the club with nimble malice.

Again, the predator dodged the blow, but the blur of the near-miss forced her back. She melted into the shadows of the forest.

A moment later, she appeared from an unexpected direction, forcing the witch to twirl about to defend her back. The club beat empty air, for the creature had not yet attacked. The silent dog watched her quarry from where she stood in the moonlight, ice eyes full of rage and purpose. Deep-chested, shoulders undulating, she waited. Jaws gaping, she waited for the femur to grow heavy in Nedra's hand.

And the large thighbone was heavy. The instant the old woman's up-lifted arm faltered, the black dog hurtled at her.

The beast fell back again from the sweeping blow. And attacked again. And darted away. With nightmare persistence, she came after the witch, bounding in and out of the moonlight, relentless, tireless.

The aged woman huffed and panted; her entire body shook from the effort of wielding the sturdy elk bone. Soon, those frenzied fangs would tear tendon and sinew and topple her. Soon, the battering thighbone would fall to the side and razor teeth would rip flesh and arteries and taste hot blood.

Soon—it had to be soon—for the hour was long after midnight, and the eastern stars dimmed. If the murderous dog did not bring down her prey soon, morning light would replenish the witch's magic that had shattered with her glass knife. Morning light would protect her with radiant magic that the black dog could not rip with claw or fang.

Nedra Fell spied light through the trees—a sky gray as the dull side of aluminum foil—and her wrinkled face smiled. "Too—late!" Joints blazing with pain, marrows throbbing with weariness, she hacked away mightily with her femur club, gasping and cackling like a sputtering muffler, "Too—late! Ha! Too—late—for *you!*"

Desperate for the kill, the black creature howled at the brightening sky and flung herself at the witch. The bone wand smote her under the jaw, clacking her teeth together sharply, and toppling her head over tail.

Lungs aching, legs shivering, Nedra Fell hurled a harsh laugh at the raging brute twisting through the dead leaves. The bitch wrenched upright, muzzle foaming a ferment of hate and fury. Eyes of frost in a black mask of hackled fur fixed the aged woman with a look of uncanny and evil intelligence.

And then, the creature was gone.

THE UNSEEN SCENE

What is a ghost but a double, astral twin of the flesh, roaming a dark dream, where night transpires in moon smoke and star shadows, wearing your face?

1.
WOMAN MADE OF FLOWERS

*Conjured by magic to serve as the wife of a prince, the beautiful Celtic
goddess Blodeuwedd proudly bore her name: 'face of flowers.' Though
fashioned from blossoms of oak, meadowsweet and broom, she knew
her own mind and had her own desires. Alas, when she insisted on
going her way with the lover of her choice, the magician who conjured
her turned her into an owl.*
—Welsh myth

On a slow bend of dirt road in the middle of a forest stood a giant statue
covered with flowers. The huge manikin, big as a parade float, had the curvaceous shape of a woman with one hand on her hip and the other behind
her head, posing like a pinup from a former era. Daffodils at the top and
sides of her head and along her shoulders created the illusion of golden,
flowing hair. Rue anemones, with their white and blush petals, filled out
her face and arms in flesh tones. Violets served for the blue of her eyes, red
wild ginger her lips, and columbines, geraniums and ferns made up the
flowing robes of her gown.

The manikin was not yet complete. The back of her body exposed a
wicker framework packed with loam waiting for insertions of flowers. Trays
of hyacinths, lilacs and crocuses sat on the grass beside a large twig-framed
sign that faced the street beneath the giantess and told passersby her name
in both runes and floral-shaped letters:

ᛋᛚᛟᛗᛖᚢᛖᛗᛗ
Blodeuwedd
[Blud—EYE—eth]
Woman Made of Flowers

Near the shoulder of the dirt road, directly alongside the Woman Made of Flowers, a ramshackle commercial enterprise squatted—a primitive souvenir stand. Handcrafted merchandise dangled from splintery rafters and eaves: gourd lanterns, bird-bone wind chimes, ritual masks of tree bark and pine cones, and poppets—dolls woven out of straw and fitted with fleshy faces carved from apples and lacquered to glossy expressions of eerie tranquility. Fronting the rickety stand, another large, twig-framed sign of colorful floral letters announced:

NEDRA'S CELTIC CURIOS & PAGAN FETISHES

This roadside attraction fronted a wide yard of tangled weeds infested with stone garden gnomes, eroded, moss-covered statuettes chipped to almost featureless rock. A winding gravel path, studded with thistles, crossed the yard to an old trailer home under the wall of the forest. A rain barrel, perched atop the tin roof beside a crooked stovepipe, wore a shawl of ivy.

The trailer home had occupied this site a long time, long enough for creepers to cover all of it and for the blocks on which it rested to sink out of sight, woven over with vines. More poppets hung in the rusty-framed windows, and above the dented aluminum door, a single nail affixed a dried-out branch, silver as driftwood and dripping gold mistletoe.

The door opened, and a young woman in a nightgown as archaic and simple as a burial shroud appeared, blinking wearily into the morning light. "Neddie?" She brushed tousled red hair from her eyes, and her elfin face, pouty with sleep, scanned the empty yard. Startling green eyes, ethereal cheekbones and slender form hinted at beauty, and she could have been lovely if not for her slouched posture, lank hair and disheveled demeanor, which diffused her attractiveness to plainness.

Yawning, the rumpled teen descended barefoot down three steps of gray planks and crossed the yard. She stepped absent-mindedly over scattered gnomes and around whopping weeds. At the Woman Made of Flowers, she called, "Neddie—you in there?"

She reached among the ferns at the side of the towering manikin and opened a door-sized section of the wicker scaffolding. Visible in the mottled light, stacks of peat bricks lay scattered beside various gardening tools.

A rectangular depression in the ground from which the bricks of peaty loam had been cut occupied the center of an otherwise empty interior.

The sleepy teenager peered into the hole. By dappled light, she saw a root-cellar door with a rope handle. A large rock atop the door held it firmly closed.

"Neddie!" she hollered, shutting the fern-covered hatch. She shuffled toward the roadside stand. "Bus is coming."

From the side entry, she glanced over an interior of pumpkin rattles, walnut shell babies, tree bark shields painted with Celtic knots, drums made from oak boles, and numerous straw poppets with wizened faces of apple flesh. She rubbed sleep from her eyes as she left the cluttered stand and strolled across the yard to the forest.

Smoky light filled the woods. The rising sun had burned off most of the morning mist and charged the air with shimmering gold dust and a fragrance of grassy resins and dew. Birdcalls trilled and chimed. Butterflies bopped among wildflowers and along the mossy banks of a creek. The creek itself stumbled noisily over stones rolled smooth as eggs.

She raised her voice louder, "Neddie! Come on. I got to get."

Across a silt bar slippery with watercress, she forded the creek. A trail penetrated bulrushes on the far side and led into a tunnel of honeysuckle and through draperies of willows to a forest glade. Pines—tall, dark, hooded druids—surrounded the clearing. In the middle, leaning sunlight illuminated a broad tree stump. An old woman in a brown sack dress sat with her back against the stump, stiff legs outstretched, eyes closed, wrinkled mouth slack.

"Neddie?" The teenager approached the old woman warily. This was not the first time she had found her grandmother asleep outdoors beside her ritual stump. The witch was old. How old the young woman had no idea, though she was sure those rheumy blue eyes had seen a world without cars and airplanes.

Gingerly, she touched the knobby shoulder and, when the crone didn't stir, nudged her.

Nedra sagged to one side, propped up by the big elk thighbone that she still grasped in one hand.

Reluctantly, the teen leaned closer and listened for breathing. She heard nothing, only the busy chatter of birds from the forest. Having anticipated this dread day for so very long, she calmly placed two fingers to the side of the old woman's neck, vainly searching for a pulse.

Sadness wafted through her and flitted away. There followed a moment of curious contemplation. Now that the morbid event so direly anticipated had actually occurred, she felt less grief than relief.

She would not have to worry anymore about losing Nedra. Her grandmother was gone, and darkness had not descended upon the world. The morning ventured on brightly: birds darted through the clearing, bees bobbled among clover, and clouds soared into the vast blue, escorting a new season across the countryside. Nothing had changed.

She sighed and gathered a double handful of dead leaves. Muttering a prayer under breath, she covered Nedra's face with leaves.

The witch sputtered and pushed upright, swatting the leaves from her face. "What's *this*?" she cried with alarm. "What's *this*?" Nedra blinked blearily at her surprised granddaughter.

Abruptly, the old woman's expression sharpened. "Flannery Lake!" She spit leaf bits and wiped her mouth. "I'm not dead. Ha! Not yet, Flower Face."

The witch's laugh collapsed to a moan, and she rolled over and slumped to the ground. Flannery stooped to help her, and the hag waved her off.

"Oh, child, leave me be."

Flannery ignored her grandmother's plea and grabbed the old woman under her shoulders. "Upsy daisy, Neddie."

With ease, Flannery lifted the elder to her feet, and Nedra groaned. "Oh, these aching bones. Don't hurry me so."

"School day, Neddie."

"School?" Nedra twisted her head around to give her granddaughter a scurrilous look. "What's school to you, Flower Face? Let me sit a spell and pull soul and body together."

"Kettle's on the fire." Flannery urged the old woman to keep walking. "Come inside, have some tea."

A horrid snarl turned Flannery's head, and she grabbed tightly at her grandmother. At the edge of the sunny clearing, a black dog big as a wolf glared at them with vicious intent.

"Scram, you!" Flannery yelled. She snatched the elk femur from beside the tree stump and waved the big bone at the mongrel. "Get away from here. Beat it!"

The black dog bristled, and its snarl deepened to a growl.

Laughter glittered in Nedra's eyes, and she tugged at Flannery's arm. "Come along, child. You won't scare that bitch."

Flannery followed her grandmother, keeping a wary eye on the violent cur watching from the forest. "I never seen that dog around here before."

"You wouldn't." On the uneven ground that sloped to the creek, Nedra reached back and took her granddaughter's hand. "She's Death. Death herself come for me."

The entire walk back to the trailer home, Flannery threw nervous glances over her shoulder. That was the largest mixed breed she'd ever seen. She helped her grandmother up the sagging steps and through the door to their home and looked around for the black dog, elk thighbone gripped securely in both hands.

The country road stretched emptily to where it cut into the dark green pines and spruce. A brace of doves alighted on the shanty roof of Nedra's souvenir stand. Butterflies flurried around the Woman Made of Flowers and through the sunbeams in the woods across the road. No other creatures crossed her sight.

2.
BLACK DOG

Why the dog? Like Anubis, dog companion of Thoth, Egyptian god of the dead—like Cerberus, guard dog of Hades—the dog is death.
—Robert Graves, *The White Goddess*

Flannery entered the trailer home and leaned the big thighbone beside the door. She had to bow her head to pass under a low ceiling crowded with sheaves of drying herbs, mobiles of bird bones and feathers, and numerous dangling poppets with lifelike faces.

A worktable occupied most of the front room. Its naked boards displayed poppets and gourd masks in various stages of assembly among their raw materials: straw bundles, twine, toad skins, snake vertebrae, raven claws and a bat's skull with its diabolic grin.

"Let me get you something hot to drink," Flannery said, following Nedra into the narrow kitchen. Morning light, curling to rainbows in the thick glass of the windows, sparkled on the white ceramic sink and its gleaming gargoyle faucet. "You shouldn't go to the altar at night, Neddie." Flannery spoke over her shoulder to her grandmother, who sat in a cane chair, chin in palm, elbow resting on a kitchen table of varnished maple. Tacked to the wall behind her, crewelwork in a frame of acorn shells declared:

History is Nature's orphan.

"It's cold at night," Flannery continued. She placed teacup and saucer before her grandmother. "If you catch a chill at your age—" With a dismal shake of her head, she admonished the old woman, then snapped a small cluster of buds from one of the hanging sheaves. She crumbled those herbs into a glass teapot on the table. Behind her, the gently steaming kettle atop the wood stove huffed hot vapors that tightened into vividly staring faces with wee expressions of impish beauty.

Nedra noticed the vaporous creatures, rubbed her face wearily and mouthed a silent chant. The rays of sunlight in the kitchen flexed as if inside a gem, and the grinning pixie faces blurred to mere steam.

Flannery, unaware of the vaporous apparitions, removed the kettle from the stove and poured its hot water into the waiting vessel. The brew swirled up murky green.

"It's only April," Flannery went on. "Too early for outdoor rituals. You could get sick."

"I'm not going to get sick. I'm going to *die*."

Flannery took down a fishbowl of cookies, lidded with a scrap of calico and twine, and brought it to the table. "Everybody's dying. So what's the hurry?"

"I'm in no hurry, child." The witch raised her white eyebrows in agreement. "That's why I worked the altar last night. It's time I act boldly, because Death is getting impatient with me. You saw the black dog."

"That was just a dog, Neddie." Flannery poured tea into her grandmother's cup. "Don't get weird on me now."

"I tell you, Flower Face, that is *the* black dog." She immersed her wrinkled face in the steam rising from the teacup. "The Theena Shee sent her for me."

Flannery gave her grandmother an irritated look and removed the cloth lid from the cookie bowl. "Got to go to school, grandma. The Theena Shee can wait." She removed several cookies and arranged them on the saucer around the teacup.

"Be careful, child." The crone watched her darkly. "The black dog got a good look at you. The Theena Shee would be happy taking a young thing in my place."

Flannery gazed upward in feigned dismay. "It's not elves I have to worry about, Neddie." She fit the scrap of calico over the cookie bowl and secured the twine. "I take another skip day, I won't graduate."

The old woman opened her mouth to say something, but the girl had already turned away.

"Try and stay inside today, Neddie. We'll work in the garden when I get back." Flannery hurried through a nutshell curtain that separated the kitchen from the back of the trailer home, and the strands clacked loudly behind her, silencing any protest the old woman might have made.

Alone in her room, the teenager breathed a peevish sigh. Flannery didn't care for the old religion or the childish bric-a-bracs and curios Nedra fashioned for her pathetic souvenir stand. In fact, Flannery didn't care about much of anything.

Other than a prism mobile that hung in a sunny window, her sleeping quarters were as bare as her heart: no posters, pictures, or stuffed animals. No bookshelves. No clock or calendar. Her neatly made cot looked spare as a prison bunk. The flimsy wood table that served as her desk held only a glass oil lamp. On the well-worn straw carpet, her denim book bag lay unopened from the day before.

Streaks of rainbows fluttered through the small room from the prisms turning in a window breeze. Like delicate creatures, they swarmed around Flannery as she opened a narrow closet and quickly selected from her homespun wardrobe baggy brown trousers and a rumpled pullover once green now almost gray.

She dressed quickly and morosely, not wanting to go to school but definitely wanting to get away from her nagging grandmother. She stepped into scuffed brogans while combing her ruffled hair with the fingers of one hand and grabbing her book bag with the other. Turning to rush out of the room, she glanced quickly past the spinning colors of the dangled prisms into the nearby forest.

Cold fear rose up in her. At first, she wasn't sure why. The dark wall of pine lay shadowed against the rising sun, no different than it had looked any other spring morning. She squinted into the slant light. Then, she spotted it beside a bent hickory—the black dog, motionless and watchful as a piece of darkness the night had left behind.

3.
SOMETHING WRONG WITH THE KID

Love weaves the cloak of sorrow.
—ancient Irish adage

Flannery burst out the front door, leaped off the stoop, and crossed the weedy yard with graceful speed. Nimbly, she dodged the stone garden gnomes in her path, eager to get away.

Nedra came out the door waving the elk thighbone. "At least take the wand! Protect yourself!"

Flannery ran beyond the Woman Made of Flowers and shouted from out of sight, "Stay indoors!"

The big dog had spooked her, and she jogged down the middle of the dirt road, looking apprehensively into the empty forest on either side. For confidence, she swung her book bag by its strap, loose and heavy.

The black dog was nowhere in sight. The muscular bitch stalked from deeper in the woods, trailing the girl's scent. The young one smelled vulnerable—frightened. Blood-salt and flesh-heat on the light wind eddying through the pines excited the beast.

She moved closer to the briny scent until her quarry came into sight. Just out of Flannery's line of vision, the dog pursued, coursing faster as the girl ran lithely along the country road, slipping in and out of view among the trees.

The dirt road ended at a paved highway, and Flannery tossed her book bag to the ground and leaned against a rusty pole under a school bus sign sieved with bullet holes. She jammed her hands into her pockets and watched butterflies jitter in the radiant air.

The black dog glided out of the forest, her attention fixed on the teenager standing in sunlight smoky with pollen. Her breathing tautened to a snarl as she closed in on the daydreaming girl.

Under a turn of wind, the sunlit wisps of pollen behind Flannery swirled with impish faces. The black dog paused. Her growl disappeared into sudden engine noise as a school bus whooshed around the bend. Hissing a loud whine, the bus braked to a stop. Doors clacked open, and the imp faces slurred away in the back draft. Flannery hoisted her book bag and boarded.

She slouched toward the rear of the almost empty bus, past two younger students. Children of affluent farmers from farther down the paved road, they usually drove to school with older siblings. For whatever reason, today they rode the school bus. One of them gawked at her, fascinated by Flannery's rustic attire and wild hair. The other whispered, "Don't look into her eyes. She's a witch."

"Nah." The gawker shook her head and whispered back, "Her grandma's the witch. She's just a retard."

Flannery scowled at the kids—"Boo!"—and they pulled away with startled cries and flurried giggles.

As usual, Flannery strode to the very back, threw her book bag on the floor and plopped down next to the window. She spotted the black dog standing among the trees, staring at her.

Fear tightened the knuckles of her spine, and she stared absently while springwoods scrolled by. She tried not to think about the dog. The bus stopped, and two more kids got on. Her mind roved ahead to what the day offered: a math quiz and a social studies presentation on the origins of World War One, neither of which she was prepared for.

Newly turned fields slid past, and farmhouses gradually gave way to suburban tracts. The interior of the bus filled with more kids. None sat near her. A few looked askance in her direction, and some openly mocked her among themselves for her hand-stitched clothes and sullen demeanor. She ignored them.

Out the window, on a wide street of sycamores, she noticed the black dog standing in the driveway of a well kept home. The bitch watched her with baleful pale eyes as the bus rolled on. Flannery straightened and heaved around to peer out the back window, stunned that the creature could have come so far so fast. The big dog kept her gaze fixed on her until the bus turned a corner.

By then, most of the seats had filled, and no one sat near Flannery. A few jeering faces sporadically looked her way. She paid them no heed. She was wondering if this black dog was the same animal that had confronted her in the woods earlier.

The bus stopped before a beige brick house fronted with poplar trees and a personalized mailbox that read: HUBERT. A bespectacled, neatly groomed boy with a heavy backpack walked his bicycle down the driveway toward the bus. An older version of himself in a business suit, with brief-case in hand, waved to him from the carport and got into a blue compact. From the front door, a woman wearing a floral housecoat rushed out wagging a bag lunch.

The busload of kids hooted and hollered with derision and began chanting, "Chester Hubert! Chester Hubert!" The bus driver motioned for them to quiet down and got out to help Chester with his bicycle. One of the older kids lowered a window and yelled, "Hey, Hubert! Give us some love!"

Chester waved cheerfully to his fans in the bus, took the lunch bag from his mother and kissed her on the cheek. Whistles and laughter erupted from his schoolmates, and he hurried to mount his bicycle on the rack at the front of the bus.

"Chet, Chet, teacher's pet. Biggest geek we ever met!" Spitballs and paper airplanes flew from the younger kids as Chester got on board. He made his way down the aisle, smiling and nodding easy as a politician on a campaign bus.

"Pipe down!" the bus driver barked, climbing back behind the wheel.

Chester grinned at his detractors with self-deprecating humor and held up his lunch bag. "Trade anybody? Got tuna and chunky peanut butter. On pumpernickel with ketchup."

To a chorus of groans, he moved toward the back of the bus fending off flying rubber bands. He dropped his ponderous pack onto the back seat and sat next to Flannery.

"Hey," he greeted.

Flannery, who was searching for the black dog, had not turned her face from the window during Chester's boisterous entry, and she continued to ignore him.

"Okay if I sit here?" he asked.

Oblivious to him, Flannery gazed out the window as the bus moved on.

"Dumb question," Chester acknowledged.

Flannery watched suburban houses float past.

"So, uh, well . . . " Chester leaned forward to catch Flannery's eye, but her stare didn't budge from the window. "I, uh, was wondering if you're going with anybody."

Flannery turned, just now registering he had sat beside her. "What do you want, Chester?"

"Chet," he corrected. "Call me Chet. Uh, I was just asking if you have a date for the spring dance."

Flannery returned her attention to the window. "I'm not going."

"You don't have a date?" Chet spoke excitedly. "All right! Great. I mean, that's okay. That's good. Maybe then you and I—we could go together."

Flannery intently watched as the bus turned onto a commercial street. She scanned a strip mall.

Chet babbled on, "Hey, this would just be for fun. You know, just cause these are our last weeks in high school and all. Something to do. No big deal."

Flannery, relieved to see no sign of the black dog, sat back in her seat. She met the expectation on the shining face of the kid beside her with a baffled scowl. "What?"

Chet's cheeks ballooned, and he exhaled a huge sigh—then shrugged and sought a new approach: "We've known each other forever. And we've spoken—what? Maybe six times in thirteen years?" He perceived Flannery's blank look and lost his train of thought. "Yeah, well, this isn't exactly easy for me to say. I can feel my ears burning. They're red, right? They feel red. Okay, I might as well just say it." He sucked in a deep breath. "I've always admired you, Flannery."

"Admired?" She gave him a cynical, sidelong glance.

Chet nodded energetically. "Other kids think you're off, because you never say anything in class, never hang out with anybody—and you wear these—your homemade clothes. But I've seen you on the playground feeding birds and squirrels. You're into nature. I admire that."

Flannery inclined her head toward the window and looked at the city streets.

"Uh, so you think maybe we could go to the dance together?" Chet asked hopefully. "I know it's short notice. But this could be our last chance to get to know each other."

With her face against the window, she rolled her eyes as they pulled into the parking lot of the city high school. The vehicle slowed to a stop, and she snagged her book bag and got to her feet with the other kids.

"I know I sprang this on you suddenly," Chet said, his magnified eyes glinting earnestly. "Don't say no right away. Think about it."

She shouldered past him and shoved her way through the kids waiting to disembark, provoking a chorus of chafed voices: "Hey!—Watch it, vampire slayer!—Downshift, girl!"

Chet crawled across the backseat, opened the side window and called to her when she walked by: "Flannery!"

She looked up and grimaced into the glare reflecting off his eyeglasses.

"Let's talk about it at lunch," he said and wagged his lunch bag. "Kohlrabi brioche and star fruit?"

Squinting a discouraging frown, she hurried off.

4.
SMACKED

Death hides in the open.
—The Black Book of Caermathon

Flannery walked quickly, afraid Chet was going to apologize again and call even more attention to her across the schoolyard. In her eagerness to get away from the sunstruck lenses on the expectant face leaning out the window, she dashed behind the bus and into the parking lot.

Chet's jaw dropped, and his eyes bugged. From his higher vantage, he could see another school bus pulling out, and he bawled, "Flannery!"

She glowered at him, annoyed—and rushed directly into the path of the accelerating bus. With a heavy thud, the impact sent her flying across the asphalt, limbs flinging, body rolling and bouncing like tumbleweed.

The school bus screeched, and students screamed and shouted.

Chet bolted from his seat and pushed his way through onlookers into the parking lot.

Flannery laid sprawled on her back, eyes half-lidded, showing zombie whites.

She snapped alert and found herself surrounded by shoes and sneakers of encroaching kids. The air resounded with their dismay and fright: "Damn! Did you see her fly?"—"She walked right into it!"—"Retard wasn't even looking."—"She was talking to Hubert."—"Is she dead?"

"It's my fault!" Chet's hysterical voice rose above the other excited voices.

The voices muted, and a storm wind whistled loudly. A pair of scuffed brogans joined the footwear surrounding Flannery. The sibilant wind faded into eerie silence, and Flannery stared above the scuffed brogans at her own baggy brown trousers and gray rumpled pullover. For an instant, she glimpsed herself standing astride herself, peering down, placid and curious.

The whole world spun dizzily, and she closed her eyes. When she opened them again, she was standing among the other kids, gaping at her fallen body on the asphalt. Astonished, Flannery looked around at the gabbling students and the shocked bus driver restraining an agitated Chet. They were talking, but she couldn't hear them.

"Hey!" she called. "What's happening?"

No one responded—because no one saw her. They stood gawking at her still body. She bent over and touched her senseless face. Her flesh felt warm and dewy.

A furious growl jerked her around. The black dog charged across the parking lot, fangs flashing.

Flannery stood up with a shriek, turning to the gathered crowd for help. No one else saw the attack dog—or her. She grabbed at the nearest kids, and even as she reached out, the dog collided with her.

Hurtling backward under the impact, she fell to the ground at the feet of the unsuspecting students. The dog's slobbering jaws snapped savagely for her throat. Frantically, she took hold of the beast's thick neck and held off her murderous jaws.

A roaring engine muffled the brute's rabid barking. From the corner of her startled eyes, she glimpsed a sleek black motorcycle slash across the parking lot. The blond rider in dark glasses wore a face of dangerous beauty, very like the impish visages that had been secretly watching her.

The bike slid sideways, abruptly stopping alongside the struggling girl, and the rider's leg swung out and kicked the black dog with the heel of a snakeskin boot. The creature tumbled away, yelping sharply.

"Come on!" The stranger extended a gloved hand, and Flannery stared up at her rescuer, astonished by his outlandish attire: kidskin pants woven along the seams with colorful Celtic knots, thongs of rawhide crisscrossing a brawny chest tattooed with blue runes, and silver charms piercing ears, eyebrows and lip.

5.
THE OTHERWORLD

The Greek word mechane, *the source of our word* machine *and origin of* machination, *means to trick—and so, whenever the fairy employ machines, they use them to deceive.*
—Roger Pelion, *Secrets of the Fairy*

Flannery hesitated to take the stranger's gloved hand, alarmed by his pirate beauty. Then, the black dog scrambled upright, eyes flaring, jaws grinding. And Flannery swiftly clasped the tattooed arm. The biker pulled her off the ground and smoothly swung her behind him onto the motorcycle.

With concussive thunder, the bike jumped away.

The black dog, barking vehemently, chased the fleeing motorcycle across the parking lot. Leaping into the air, the animal stretched monstrously, elongating like a demonic cartoon to a surreal blur of slashing claws and hot fangs.

Flannery cast a terrified look over her shoulder. Claws cut through her streaming hair, and sharp teeth gnashed inches away. The deathly shadow fell back, smearing flat across the asphalt, a long fierce smudge black as a tire burn.

As the motorcycle flowed into street traffic, a wailing ambulance flew past in the opposite direction. Moments later, the emergency vehicle swerved to the curb of the schoolyard and pulled up short beside Flannery's rag doll body.

The principal and school security herded most of the students into the building. Chet insisted on staying with Flannery and giving the police a statement. He lingered afterward and watched with a poisoned expression as the paramedics loaded Flannery's unconscious body onto a gurney.

"It's my fault," he told the nearest police officer. "Book me on negligent endangerment."

"And you are?" the officer inquired.

"He's Chester Hubert," a second officer answered, stepping out from behind the ambulance and waving off the first cop. "I already got his statement. He was in the parked bus when it happened."

"It's my fault," Chet asserted. "I distracted her. This wouldn't have happened except for me."

The officer pointed with his chin to the school. "Counselors are waiting for you in there, kid."

"No." Chet spoke loudly, to hear himself above his rushing blood. "You have to book me. I'm responsible for what happened."

Chet watched the ambulance doors close and the red flashers spin. The wail of the siren cut through him so sharply, he thought he was going to vomit. He scurried around to the front of the parked bus and unracked his bicycle. Keeping the bus between him and the huddled squad cars, he hopped on his bike and pedaled furiously across the parking lot in pursuit of the speeding strobe lights.

Further away than he could ever hope to pedal—or even imagine—Flannery and the blond biker cruised along a country road through tigery shadows of trees. Overhead, fluffy clouds trod the sky like sheep. She pressed her face into the rushing air, long red hair buffeting behind. The wind bleared her eyes, stung her face and assured her she was alive.

Urgent questions swarmed, but the bike's rocketing speed snatched her breath away and made talking hopeless. She leaned against the biker and squeezed her arms tighter about him.

He smelled tawny, like worn leather. Was she dead? Was this the afterlife: a motorcycle ride into heaven with a biker angel?

They rolled to a stop before a meadow embroidered with flowers. On a distant hill, willows glistened. A small waterfall stepped down mossy ledges like a flight of stairs and fed a brook that meandered across the meadow and disappeared into a majestic forest. A dozen young adults lounged in the low, gnarled boughs of trees. They all wore dark glasses and crazy-casual clothes and watched her with severely lovely, impish faces.

"This is a dream, isn't it?" Flannery asked when the engine noise cut off. From somewhere nearby, music lilted, forlorn and frail, riding a balmy breeze with butterflies, pollen smoke and milky tufts of dandelions. "I'm dreaming—or I'm dead and this is the next world."

"Is that what you think?" the blond rider asked, voice soft as suede. "The black dog doesn't think you're dead."

She flicked an uneasy glance down the road.

"Don't worry, Flannery." The biker nodded for her to dismount. "We don't have to run anymore."

"How do you know my name?" She got off the bike, legs humming like struck crystal from the vibrant, fast ride. "Who are you? Where are we?"

Friendly laughter rippled among the young people watching her and whispering light-heartedly to each other. "We all know you, Flannery." The rider sat back in the saddle of the machine. "And we want you to get to know us."

"I saw my body on the ground." Fear pleated Flannery's voice. "Am I dead?"

"You're in a coma." He dropped the kickstand and got off the bike. "By now, your gutsack is in a hospital bed and stuck with tubes. That's not you." Under the warm gazes and nods of his friends, he strode through the meadow's clover grass and sat on a low bough over the brook. "Come here. We're not going to eat you."

Flannery looked at the attractive, lolling youths in their careless attire and shook her head. She didn't belong with these people. Whippet-thin girls wore silk tops slashed to their navels; techno-pagan boys sported hacked manes and razor-wire fetish charms in their ears and eyebrows. They should have been smirking at her. Instead, they smiled warmly and beckoned her, "Get out of the heat and sprawl."

Flannery leveled a suspicious look at her rescuer. He reclined on a tree limb with the sinuous grace of a cat. "Who are you?"

"Arden."

She tucked in her chin. "*What* are you?"

He offered a mischievous smile and gestured at the others. "We are the Theena Shee."

"*Elves?*" Flannery blurted.

Arden winced. "We don't like that name."

"I'm dreaming." Flannery scowled with disbelief. "The bus hit me and knocked me into a dream."

"No, you're not dreaming." He said this in an indifferent voice. "The bus knocked you free of your corpse, and you're here with us now."

"With the Theena Shee?"

Arden nodded, and the others softly laughed at her glorious disbelief. "I thought the Theena Shee were a fairy tale."

"Strange world."

Flannery's knees wobbled, and she leaned back against the bike saddle and tracked the landscape with a startled vigilance. This peaceful meadow intruded among primeval woods of enormous trees where perpetual night lingered. She didn't want to stare too deeply into those gloomy timberlands, afraid she'd spot the black dog roving there.

She focused on the tilting meadow. Small fork-tailed birds laced the air and glistening dragonflies zigged and zagged. Far off, indigo mountains rose to crystal crags and blue snow bowls. Waterfalls descended those dark walls of rock and dissolved into rainbows.

"What is this place?" she asked hollowly, trying to untangle her emotions—her fear and awe—from her disbelief. "This can't be real."

"This is the Otherworld, Flannery." Arden addressed her matter-of-factly. "The world behind the world you know. This is where we live. This is where you can live, too—if you come with us."

She peered more carefully at the meadow, searching for the flaw in her dream. Her uneasiness dissolved among the daisies, pink clover and deep-blue gentians. "It's so beautiful . . . "

"Come on, then." He waved his hand over his head in a summoning flourish. "Join us."

Flannery tugged at her hair till her scalp hurt, convincing herself she was awake. "I don't believe this is happening."

"Look at us." Arden stood upon the bough, arms outstretched. "Don't you recognize us in your heart? We are your heart's choice."

"Choice?" Flannery cocked her head. "You mean, I can go back? Back to my body?"

In playful imitation, Arden cocked his head and lifted an eyebrow above his dark glasses. "You want to go back?"

"Yes."

"You weren't very happy back there." He hopped off the bough and offered his gloved hand. "Decide later. Come on. Let me introduce you to the others."

Flannery decided this *was* a dream. It had to be. Everything was too achingly beautiful. Better to share this gorgeous dream, she thought, than wake up alone in a hospital ward—or, worse, a morgue. With fear and longing, she strode into the fairy landscape and the warm embrace of the wickedly lovely people.

6.
ONE CRAZY WITCH

Long and white are my fingers—as the ninth wave of the sea.
—Hanes Blodeuwedd (The Poem of Flower Face)

Chet stood beside an empty crash cart in a clinic corridor talking to a doctor with porcupine hair, a big potato nose and delicate, gold wire spectacles. A paisley of hospital noise imprinted the medicinal air, and a speaker voice clamored, "Doctor Antone, report to Neurology. Doctor Antone to Neuro."

"That's me." The doctor backed away. "I've got to go."

"Wait," Chet pleaded feverishly, looking as if he himself might require urgent care at any moment. "Is she going to be all right?"

"Internal organs are uninjured and surprisingly no bones are broken," the doctor reported, edging backward. He paused and lowered his voice all the way to a whisper. "But she sustained head trauma. She could wake up in five minutes. She may never wake again. I've got to go."

Chet stood nervously before the open door of the observation unit where the emergency staff had placed Flannery. Electronic chirpings and an antiseptic taint wafting from the room heightened his anxiety about actually facing her and seeing the damage he had caused. Bracing himself, he stepped through the doorway.

The sight of Flannery lying on her back in a hospital bed, glucose drip-tube stuck in one arm, monitor cuff on the other, left him aghast. Her hair looked red as fire, her flesh gray as rain. For a freaky instant, he thought he had arrived at the precise moment of her death. Then, he noticed the green spikes on the monitor recording the tread of her heart.

Slowly, he approached and stood at her bedside gazing down at her slack features. She didn't appear as though she were peacefully slumbering. Jaw hanging loose, mouth agape, skewed lids exposing the whites of her eyes, she looked knocked senseless. "I'm so sorry." He stifled a sob. "All these years—I wanted to talk—I just never had the nerve. And then, when I finally—" He swallowed another sob and removed his eyeglasses to wipe away tears with the back of his hand.

Behind him, Nedra Fell, in her hempen gown and cobweb hair, stood in the doorway. She didn't enter.

Chet continued, "If you can hear me, Flannery, know I'm really sorry. I should've let you go. You wouldn't be here now if I had let you go. It's all my fault. And I'm sorry, really sorry. Please, wake up. I won't ever talk to you again. I promise. I'll leave you alone. Just wake up."

He bent close and kissed her forehead.

A brusque voice directly behind him asked, "Who are you?"

Chet whirled. The gnomic old woman glowering at him with arctic wolf eyes hovered like an apparition. "Me?" He laid a hand over his scampering heart, his cheeks blazing with the realization the crone had heard every word he'd said. "I—I'm a friend of Flannery's from school."

"Flannery doesn't have any friends." With startling eyes of smashed ice, Nedra inspected the agitated teen who had just kissed her comatose granddaughter. "What's your name?"

"Chester?" Chet followed up more firmly, "Chester Hubert. I—I've known Flannery since we were in kindergarten."

The crumpled face, enclosed by thick mats of tangled spider webs, squinted skeptically. "She never mentioned you."

"Oh, no way she could," he gusted with embarrassment. "I mean—I never spoke with her. Not really. Not until today, that is."

"Unlucky for her." Nedra stepped closer, scowling ominously. "Chester Hubert."

"I'm sorry." His voice wobbled. "I mean, I'm so very sorry about what happened."

The old woman inched very close to Chet, and he backed away, taking with him a whiff of her scent, something fragrantly sad, like November rain. "It was *your* fault."

"I think it was. Yes." Chet nodded vigorously. "I know it was my fault. I called to her from the bus . . . I—I just wanted to ask her to the spring dance—I . . . "

Nedra pointed at her granddaughter with a finger brown as a root. "She's lying there because of you, Chester Hubert."

"I told the police . . . "

Chet backed into the bed, and Nedra pinned him against the cool metal of the railing. "Do you love her?"

"Love?" He gawked. "Well, uh—I've admired her for years—from afar, but I never really . . . "

She bit off each word with her reptilian lips, "Do—you—*love*—her?"

He offered a small nod. "Yes."

The crinkled face relaxed. "Then, you can save her," she said gently.

"What?"

The crone stepped back a pace so that he could plainly reckon the full length of her uncanny presence, from her voodoo frenzy of tangled hair and the grim radiation of her weather-beaten face to the medieval memory of her hempen gown and rope sandals. "Do you know who I am?"

"You're Flannery's grandmother?" Chet piped, then forced himself to speak more huskily, "I've seen you at school—picking her up when we were little . . . "

"I am Nedra Fell," she interrupted forcefully. "I am a Wiccan priestess."

"You—you're what?"

"I am a witch."

"Oh."

She pushed closer and informed him confidentially, "Flannery's soul has been knocked loose from her body. And if she is not returned to her flesh soon, she will die."

The shimmery intensity of the crone's stare filled Chet with cold dread, and he trembled before the conspicuousness of her lunacy. "The doctor said . . . "

"The doctor does not know Flannery." Nedra spoke with demented urgency. "I tell you, she will die unless you fetch her soul from the Otherworld."

"Me?" Chet's shrill eyes grew larger. "You're the witch . . . "

"I am old." With this unhappy admission, Nedra's whole body seemed to deflate, and she added in a tone of bitter, self-scorn, "If I go to the Otherworld, Flannery and I will both be lost."

Chet sidled past the shrunken madwoman and drifted toward the door. "I'm really sorry about what happened."

"You, Chester Hubert, you are her only chance of coming back." The witch floated after him. "If you don't work the Fetch, the Theena Shee will hold her in the Otherworld until her body dies."

"Who?"

"The Theena Shee. The spirit people." She put her misshapen hand on Chet's shoulder and stopped his retreat. "What is your ancestry?"

"What?"

"Who are your ancestors?" She sidestepped Chet and blocked him from exiting the room. "Hubert—what is that? French?"

"Uh, yes." He gave his head a determined nod while his jittery eyes gauged the distance to the open door. "My dad's grandparents were from Brittany. Northwest France."

"You have Celtic blood." She sized him up with an air of artful scrutiny. "You could find the Theena Shee in the Otherworld. They would recognize you."

The manic glee in the professed witch's face sparked genuine fright in Chet, and he budged past her gruffly. "Look, I've got to go." He darted out of the room.

Nedra Fell, tottering backward, shouted into the hallway. "Chester Hubert! Only you can save her!"

7.
HOME INVADER

Make dread, thy heart, for the witch comes in the night.
—Sir Thomas Browne, *Garden of the Witch*

At the dinner table, Chet had no appetite. He leaned his fork against a pancetta-wrapped baked potato and stared at it as if it were some cumbersome object. His parents, Elliot and Lena, shared concerned looks.

Elliot ate his meal as he did every evening at the linen-draped dining table formally set with rose-print dishware and crystal goblets. His wife Lena, however, picked sporadically at the food on her plate and, no longer able to watch her son gazing disconsolately at his untouched meal, finally spoke up, "Chester, we know you think otherwise, but what happened today is not your fault."

Chet addressed the immovable potato, "Then, who is to blame?"

"The young lady for not looking where she was going," Elliot answered around a mouthful of roast loin of pork.

"Dad, her name is Flannery." Chet forked the potato so hard the tines shoved all the way through and clacked against the plate. "And she *wasn't* looking—because I distracted her."

"Flannery Lake," Lena spoke up brightly, cutting off any reply her husband might have made to Chet's angry fork. "She's the girl who lives with her grandmother. I've seen the old woman at school a few times. Nedra Fell. Quite a character. I think she sells her own crafts."

"I know her," Elliot recalled, waving a forkful of garlic mash with pear sauce. "She has a doohickey stand out on Old Mill Road, sells voodoo dolls and stuff. You know, the place with that big statue of flowers that looks like a woman."

"That's her stand?" Lena absently pierced a single pea. "I haven't been out that way in years. How does she manage to set that up every spring?

41

What a remarkable green thumb."

Elliot reached for another scallion biscuit from the basket beside the gravy boat and casually asked his son, "What happened to Flannery's parents?"

"I don't know," Chet answered sullenly.

"They died in an accident," Lena informed the table. "Car crash—years ago, when Flannery was very young, two or three."

Elliot frowned at his son frowning at his food.

"Mothers talk," Lena explained and poured a dollop of shallot sauce onto the untouched slab of pot roast on her son's plate. "One of the mothers works in the school office and must have seen the records."

Elliot noticed Chet's lips tighten and his eyes narrow a critical stare at Lena. "You're right, son. This is pure gossip. We shouldn't be talking about that poor girl when we really don't know anything about her."

The penciled lines of Lena's eyebrows lifted defensively. "I was just relating what I'd heard."

"That, I'd say, is a pretty fair definition of gossip, Lena." Elliot turned to his son with a smug expression of complicity. "Listen to me, Chester. Accidents happen. That bus driver is more to blame than . . . "

The doorbell chimed insistently. Elliot looked to his wife and son to see if they were expecting anyone. Blank stares circulated the table, and the doorbell continued to bong maniacally.

The convulsive ringing persisted as Elliot put down his knife and fork, removed the napkin from his lap, and rose from the table. "All right, already!" he griped, striding into the foyer past the antique cloak rack, umbrella stand, and a parlor vase stuffed with decorative feather-blooms of pampas grass. "I hear you!"

The front door swung open on an old woman with a face the color of dead leaves and hair white and flamboyant as steam. In her big-knuckled hand, she wielded a stout thighbone the size of a shillelagh. "Where is Chester?" she asked gruffly.

"We're having dinner." Elliot observed the woman's coarse gown with its needlework along the neckline that resembled runes and other heathen symbols, and he surmised, "You're that girl's grandmother. I'm sorry about . . . "

Nedra grimaced angrily. The femur wand in her hand punched forward, striking Elliot between the eyes with a resounding *thwack*! He dropped like a bag of bones, and the crone stepped over his collapsed body and stormed into the house, shouting, "Chester Hubert!"

The crazed hag stalked into the dining room brandishing her femur wand, and Lena leaped up, toppling her chair. The witch pointed the sturdy thighbone at Chet, who sat open-mouthed before her wrathful cry, "You!"

"Elliot!" Lena screeched.

Nedra hammered the dining room table with the femur wand, shattering a serving platter and scattering peas and pearl onions like shrapnel. "My granddaughter is dying because of you!"

Lena hollered again, "Elliot!"

"How can you sit here?" Nedra jabbed the femur at Chet. "How can you stuff your gullet while she lies dying in the hospital?"

From behind the old woman, Elliot staggered into the dining room, hair disarrayed, expression dazed yet smoldering.

"Mrs. Fell—please!" Lena waved both arms, hoping to distract the madwoman from Elliot's wobbly approach.

Nedra ignored the frightened woman and held Chet in her livid gaze. "I told you what you have to do, young man."

Elliot seized the old woman from behind, and she bucked in his arms and howled with rage. "Release me!"

Grunting and huffing, Elliot dragged the struggling witch from the dining table.

"The Fetch!" Nedra wailed, legs kicking. "Chester! Only you can work the Fetch!"

Lena hurried around the table, hands meekly outstretched toward the grappling couple, feeling both alarmed and reassured by her husband's stern strength. "Don't hurt her, Elliot."

"How dare you barge in here and attack my family?" Elliot spoke through a clenched jaw, striving as arduously to contain his rage as restrain the manic intruder. "I should call the police." With great effort, he pulled her twisting and jerking out of the room.

"You love her!" Nedra shouted from the foyer, her grievous voice booming through the house.

Lena turned toward her son with a wide-eyed look of dismay. He didn't notice. He was staring stunned across the havoc of the dining room table at where the witch had stood accusing him.

In the foyer, Elliot managed to open the front door with one frantic hand. He leaned his shoulder into the thrashing old woman and shoved her out into the night. "If you don't leave at once," he warned, standing squarely in the doorway, "I won't care anymore about what happened to your granddaughter. I'll call the police."

Nedra irately raised the femur wand, and Elliot slammed the door, leaving her standing alone under the porch light, trembling like a flame.

8.
PARTY ANIMALS

Dance, dance, dance to a Druid tune—while God sleeps
'neath the faeries' moon.
—Gwion's Riddle

Flannery and Arden lay together on a mossy bank of a brook among violets and minty grasses. Pollen mist, butterflies and aerial seeds like tufts of feathers filled the air with a dreamy, vagrant beauty, and, in the tricky waters of the brook, rainbows glinted and spiny-finned fish plunged.

Scattered across the meadow and in the sun-mottled alcoves of the surrounding forest, the Theena Shee loafed in couples and drowsy threesomes. Flannery sat up sleepily and surveyed the idyllic scene. She felt wonderful. Her crucial loserness had entirely vanished, and the isolation she had lived with all her life gone, as well. Half-smiles and nods of welcome tossed her way from these beautiful creatures banished all self-doubt.

"This is too lovely," she spoke her fear aloud once again. "It must be a dream."

"It is," Arden admitted, hands behind his head, a grass stem between his teeth. "This is the place where we dream our days away."

"How long have we been here?" She watched bright breezes drift across the broad grassland under toppling clouds—and noticed how the forest shadows had lengthened. "It seems only minutes—but already it's getting dark."

"Time moves differently in the Otherworld," Arden mumbled sleepily.

"I have to go back," Flannery decided, sitting up straighter. Her happiness collapsed into misgiving once she realized how much time had gotten away from her. "Neddie must be worried sick."

"Forget about that old witch." He sank deeper into the hummocky grass.

"She's not interested in your happiness. All she cares about is Wicca. How do you think she's lived to be so old?"

Flannery showed him her surprise. "You know my grandmother?"

"You mean your great-great-great grandmother," he mumbled from a drowsy depth. "There might be another great or two in there. Nedra Fell is a lot older than you think." He felt the pressure of her stare and sat up with a lazy sigh. "The Theena Shee know your Neddie quite well." He clenched the grass stem between his teeth and faced her, wraparound sunglasses reflecting the beautiful world darkly. "We've been doing business with that old witch since she was young as you—a very long time ago."

Flannery absorbed this news silently for a dumbfounded moment while she tried to decide how much of what she was experiencing was valid. If this wasn't a dream—if her soul had truly departed her body and trespassed the Otherworld—"Then, everything Neddie's been telling me since I was a kid is true?" Amazement teemed through her with possibilities that always before she had dismissed as fairy tales, Neddie's superstitious lore. "The Theena Shee are the first people?"

"Old as the world."

"But you wear cool outfits—" She looked out to the road, where sunlight ricocheted off the bike's chrome in crisp little rainbows. "And you ride a motorcycle?"

"All magic." He laughed, low and dark. "How better to mock the mechanical, fashion-mad world of people?"

"And this world where you live?" She admired again the sparkling brook and the distant ice-castle mountains. She felt bewitched. "This place really is the Otherworld, the paradise Neddie's been telling me about since I can remember—you know, the happy land where nobody gets sick or old?"

Arden sat back on his elbows and inhaled the spring breeze. "Every day is a good day here."

"And the dragon?" she asked with a worried furrow in her voice. "The terrible dragon that must be fed? Is that true, too?"

"Ah, the dragon." The roguery of his smile chilled her. "That's what makes our lives here so sexy."

"Then, it's true?" she asked with a frill of dread. "You lure people into the Otherworld and feed them to the dragon?"

"A few vagabonds a year," Arden conceded, his smile slipping away. "We take people that no one in the cold, dim world misses. They die merciful deaths, swift and painless, far better than the cruel fate of wandering homeless, hungry and diseased among their own people."

Flannery stood. "I think I want to go home now."

"What?" He evinced astonishment with a grin. "You're afraid I'm going to feed you to the dragon?" He dismissed that possibility with an amused chuckle. "Flannery, please. I didn't bring you here as dragon food."

"Then, why am I here?"

He rose and tossed aside the grass stem he'd been chewing. "I want you." He peeled off one of his gloves and put a gentle hand to the side of her face. "I want you for myself."

Flannery backed away. "Take me home."

His mouth turned a wry smile. "You just got here."

"You said I had a choice," Flannery challenged. "You said I could go home."

"I asked if you wanted to go home." He flapped his empty glove at the road. "You're unhappy back there, and you know it."

"I want to see Neddie."

"She'll try to talk you out of staying." Arden tilted his head back knowingly, daring her to disagree. "Wicca is all she cares about. Not you. Do you have any idea how many generations she's outlived? You're just the latest."

"Can I go home or not?"

"I'll take you home myself." He ambled toward the motorcycle and, with a jaunty wave, invited her to follow. "But first I want to show you something—" He passed a playful grin over his shoulder. "—something wonderful that I think will change your mind."

Flannery remained where she was, hands on her hips.

At the side of the road, he turned and raised his arms with the outlandish showmanship of a circus ringleader. "Our nightlife!"

When he lowered his arms, the sky darkened like houselights going down in a theater. Azure deepened to darkest blue, then indigo. Flannery craned her neck, looking for storm clouds. Instead, she witnessed the orange orb of the sun cool in the violet sky to the silver disk of a full moon.

With hushed awe, she finally accepted the fact that she was dreaming. She met Arden's pleased gaze and felt a chill, magnetic pulse of sexual force throb across the space that separated them. She figured if she was going to dream, why hold back? Anxiety and uncertainty dismissed, she climbed the moonlit embankment to his motorcycle.

The others in the meadow were already gone when she mounted the bike behind Arden. In the opal light of the moon, even the ancient and ominous forest appeared lovely, full of scintillant depths, a dark jewel under the starry sky, its interior ghostly, faceted like a shadowy crystal.

The engine revved with a growl percussive as a jackhammer, and they rode off on a molten road under the giant moon. She hugged the sturdy biker, her dream-lover, and marveled at the ingenuity of her comatose brain. The blurred speed of their ride struck her in the chest, and she clung tighter to the handsome demon rider, afraid she might wake up.

Like flickering flames, the dazzling woods flew by on either side. The road seemed to disappear entirely, and they glided as spirits through spectral groves of moonstruck trees.

The roar of the engine modulated to a growl as the bike downshifted, and they rolled to an easy stop in a large, incandescent clearing enclosed by massive trees. A high wind tossed the forest canopy so that moonfire flashed across the glade like strobe lights in a dance club.

At the center of the clearing a mammoth oak towered, its broad trunk mangled by past lightning strikes. The distorted bark, brocaded with hanging moss and scalloped fungus, bore an eerie semblance to a dragonish skull. Flannery sat mesmerized by the two dark sockets in the bole of the oak. Unearthed roots yawed like a gaping jaw.

Her fixation broke when loud and driving rock music thump-wailed from the glimmering forest, and the Theena Shee, in outfits of tattered elegance, rushed into the open, dancing frenetically, acrobatically, with a climactic abandon that rode the speed-run rhythms of the music.

Arden swept Flannery off the bike and spun her into the midst of the frenzied dancers. Theena Shee, with elvishly beautiful faces and sleek bodies, happily received her into their ecstatic crowd. For a moment, she forgot that she had agreed she was dreaming, and she gawked with a mixture of fear and wonder at the aggressive merrymakers grabbing her arms and twirling her among them.

Her fear dissolved quickly in the blissful frenzy of the celebration. She danced with Arden and the others faster and with greater abandon. Whirling, spinning, flailing with the relentless music, she glimpsed forest cubicles lit by foggy moonlight like a warren of smoky rooms. A flurry of images strobe-flashed around her, revealing ardent, momentary scenes of groping bodies, entangled limbs, passionate lovers.

Laughing at the antics of her imagination, Flannery surrendered entirely to the rapture and merged with the driving music and the laser-flickering moonlight. With joyful fervor, she and Arden danced.

The thrashing music exploded to silence. Flannery collapsed gasping and sobbing for breath in the leaf duff on the forest floor. Cradled in Arden's arms and radiant with sweat, she grinned. She was happy. And she was beautiful. Gone was her vapid plainness. The tempestuous dancing had changed her, invigorating her with a glamour she had never before known. A mysterious, vigilant luster shone in her eyes, and her flesh glowed like ivory by firelight. The planes of her face had sharpened and acquired a surprising and thoughtful intensity. Even her hair, which before had hung lankly, took on a reckless liveliness.

Morning mist swaddled the entangled, exhausted bodies of the Theena Shee where they lay strewn upon the buttress roots of the massive dragon oak. Sunlight slanted through the trees yellow as fresh-milled lumber smoking with sawdust.

Arden, true to the puckish spirit of her dream, still wore his dark glasses. He ventured a fatigued smile. "You're a passionate dancer, Flannery Lake."

"I've never had this much fun." She sighed contentedly. "I never want to wake up."

Wearily, they rose. Arden led the way across the clearing to where his motorcycle waited in a shaft of morning light hectic with butterflies. Flannery shuffled after him. Along the way, she glanced at the Theena Shee sprawled among the trees.

Most of them had passed out. But a few sat against the root ledges of the giant yews and cedars, watching her. Sunrays seeping from the branches touched their lovely faces and illuminated orange eyes, striated and sliced with vertical pupils—the eyes of beasts.

9.
A BAD PLACE

The heart has a hand—and love unties it.
—Tom o' Bedlam's Ballad

An IV tube had tangled around Flannery's throat. Her cheeks shone hot and purple. Through grimacing lips, no sound escaped. Green eyes gazed hard and horrified from their cancelled life. The agony of her death struck a blue match across Chet's heart, and he thrashed in bed, flung free of this nightmare.

The dream's frightfulness followed him to the kitchen table. He picked listlessly at his breakfast of Adzuki bean patties with a side of grilled mushrooms and tomato on fried multi-grain bread. Elliot peeked over the morning paper from the opposite side of the table and traded concerned looks with Lena as she stood at the kitchen island packing a sack lunch of cashew stuffed sweet potato balls & vegetable cake.

Chet gave up on breakfast, stood and retrieved the lunch bag from the counter.

"It's too early for the bus," Lena noted blandly, her tone free of the anxiety humming inside her.

Chet stuffed the paper sack in the ponderous backpack that hung by its straps from a kitchen chair. "I'm riding my bike to school."

"You think that's a good idea, son?" Elliot masked his worried frown with the newspaper. "You'll be heading into commuter traffic."

"I can't ride that bus," Chet stated curtly. "Not after yesterday." He kissed his mom on the cheek and slouched out of the kitchen under his heavy backpack.

"Is he going to be all right, Elliot?" Lena inquired, filled with heart-bruised longing to rush after her child and embrace him. "That crazy old woman could be stalking him. Maybe he should stay home today."

"And mope around the house all day?" Elliot snapped the creases out of the newspaper and replied without looking up, "He's better off in school. As for that nut case, Chet's old enough to watch after himself."

"Is he?" she asked, each word a throb of worry. "Mrs. Fell is violent. If she struck you, Elliot, what might she do to him? She thinks Chester's responsible for her granddaughter's accident!"

"She did whack me good." Elliot lowered the paper, revealing a contusion on his forehead that looked like a Rorschach blotch of the Bat-Out-of-Hell. "How's it look?"

Lena sucked a breath through her teeth. "I think she's dangerous. We better drive Chester to school."

"And humiliate him in front of the other kids?" Elliot ducked back into his newspaper. "Leave him alone, Lena. He has to live in the real world."

Chet pedaled his bicycle glumly through the real world, backpack strapped to the rack behind him. The school bus he usually rode passed slowly, windows down, kids leaning out and jeering: "Chet, Chet, teacher's pet!"—"Hey, lover man, you made a big *hit* with your girlfriend yesterday!"—"Ding dong the witch is dead!"

Chet stopped and watched the bus of laughing kids drive on. He pushed up his eyeglasses with his middle finger. Then, he turned his bike around and rode hard in the opposite direction.

The hospital provided a bike stand, but he didn't bother to chain his bicycle or even to take his backpack. He walked briskly through the sliding doors directly to the information desk. In the midst of his inquiry, he spotted the porcupine coiffure of Dr. Antone beyond a traffic of wheelchair outpatients and hospital volunteers.

"Doctor Antone—how's Flannery Lake doing?" Chet asked this enthusiastically, hoping to evoke an equally enthusiastic response. "The desk says she's been moved out of the ER."

Dr. Antone gave him a very hard stare. "Shouldn't you be in school?"

"I called from home, but the nurse wouldn't tell me anything," Chet lied and continued confabulating, "Flannery's my girlfriend. Is she all right?"

Behind small rectangular lenses, the doctor's dark eyes squinted, studying Chet's earnest face, deciding what could be divulged. He shook his head. "Speak to the family."

"I *am* family," Chet dissembled floridly. "We're secretly engaged. So, you can tell me. Is she all right?"

The dark eyes squinted tighter. "No, she's not all right. Her vital signs weakened overnight. If this continues, she won't last another twenty-four hours. I'm sorry."

Chet's shoulders slumped, and his whole body felt as if he were imploding as he watched the doctor walk off. Fighting this compression of dread and grief that he knew from dire experience might rebound at any instant to nausea and a puking fit, he dragged his feet toward the chiming elevators. By the time he arrived at Flannery's room, he had mastered his distress, and he peeked in anxiously, looking for the lunatic grandmother.

In one of the room's two beds, an aged woman slept curled on her side, her peach-colored hair flossy as a cloud. A kaleidoscopic pastiche of get-well cards crammed the bulletin board beside her bed. Flowers and balloons crowded her bed stand.

Beyond a curtain partition, Flannery occupied her bed like a corpse, lying on her back, perfectly straight, her brilliant red hair spread out, drying from a recent shampoo. The glucose bag and monitor alone testified she was alive and in a bad place. Her bed stand and bulletin board displayed nothing but hospital paraphernalia—a plastic vomit tray on the stand and a yellowed chapel schedule tacked to the board.

Chet leaned on the bedrail and gazed with a mix of shame and consternation at this young woman he had adored too long from afar. "Flannery," he whispered. "It's me, Chet. I'm back, because you haven't woken yet. You want to get rid of me, you better wake up."

From his shirt pocket, he removed a pen and a small notepad and, bending over the bed stand, began writing. "I'm going to make it hard on you, Flannery," he continued speaking under his breath. "I'm going to write you get well poetry. And I'm going to keep it up until you wake up and make me shut up. You hear?"

He paused in his writing, scratched out a line, chewed the end of his pen contemplatively, then scribbled again. Decisively punching the notebook with his pen, he finished. "Okay. Listen to this. It rhymes sort of." He passed the comatose girl an apologetic smile. "I'm not really good at poetry. Math is my forte. But this is from the heart. All right, here it goes—"

He sucked in a deep breath and softly read his lyric: "If you die—my life is a lie.—Come back.—I'm sorry—my love hurt you.—Come back.—My reasons are not new:—I didn't mean to love you—I know that's true—but it's you—my heart goes to."

Chet ripped out the poem and tacked it on her bulletin board, speaking with his back to her, "If you think this sucks, you better wake up soon or there's going to be a lot more."

When he turned around, Nedra Fell stood very close to him, pale, bulging eyes shining with ferocious strength.

WHEN YOU'RE HERE, YOU'RE THERE

The Otherworld exists right here, next to our world, fugitive to our senses—except in dreams, where the two worlds bleed together.

1.
TEAR IT ALL DOWN

The world is an animal.
—Marsilio Ficino

Arms crossed under his head, Arden reclined on his back beside a fumbling brook. Flannery sat nearby, atop a boulder splotched with moss, absorbing the resplendent vista. Crimson butterflies blinked among bluebells and great yellow buttercups soaking in the sun. The Theena Shee napped upon the floral slopes and under venerable trees in the mauve shade at the forest's edge. From nowhere other than her own dreaming heart, languid music riffled in the shining air carrying seed tufts and glinting spores. She felt strong and strikingly self-possessed.

"Take off your sunglasses," she told her companion.

"Hm?"

"I want to see your eyes."

He demurred with a soft shake of his head. "Too sunny."

Flannery knelt beside him, and as she reached for his dark glasses, his hand caught her wrist. "You know what you'll see."

"Show me."

Arden sat up and removed his wraparound shades. Yellow eyes blinked at her, tapered pupils constricting to vertical razor-slits. "Eyes of the beast." He hooked a self-mocking grin. "Do I frighten you?"

"No." She drew close so that their noses almost touched. "You don't frighten me. I've looked into the eyes of animals many times. They are beautiful eyes."

"You like animals. That's why you're here." Arden squinted against the daylight and pressed the dark glasses back into place. "You're happy with nature—with the original world. It's people you don't like."

57

She hesitated a moment before asserting, "I don't mind them."

"You tolerate them," Arden allowed, settling back on his elbows. "But you don't like them. And they don't like you. That's why you're here."

"I'm here because you brought me." She straddled his lap and peered at her ghostly reflection in the dark mirror of his sunglasses. "Why are *you* here?"

"This is our world."

"It's the dragon's world," she corrected and placed her hands on his shoulders, pinning him down. "I remember the fairy tales of the Theena Shee my grandma told me. If you don't feed the dragon, it will eat you. So, why do you stay? Why not live with people?"

"'Something there is that doesn't love a wall ...'" He gave her an icy smile. "Their poet Robert Frost understood."

"You could live in the forests ... "

"Polluted." He wrinkled his nose with disgust. "All of it. The water. The air. It's all tainted with the poisons of cities."

"You could help change that." She wondered why she was bothering to recruit a dream figure to participate in the real world. None of this was actual, she reminded herself. Yet, the sturdy feel of him beneath her, the tawny fragrance of him touching her face so close to his—"Don't hide in a dream. Change the real world."

"Change it?" He sat bolt upright, rolling her aside, and she toppled onto her belly and gazed up at his disdain. "I want to tear it all down—all the poisonous factories, all the stinking cities!" He rose to his knees, fists pressed against his thighs in a posture of abject futility. "But the sons of Eve and the daughters of Adam—they are killers, more fierce than the Theena Shee. We cannot fight them and win."

Marveling at his vehemence, she tried to engage a solution: "If the world knew of you ... "

"They would trap us," he interjected acerbically, "analyze us, try to make us like them. Better that we serve the dragon. It is satisfied with the people we sacrifice to it. But what satisfies people? Whole forests they devour. Whole mountains they tear apart. And still they aren't satisfied. They are rapacious monsters." He sagged, unclenching his fists. "And we fear them."

"If I'm not locked in some crazy dream," she speculated aloud, "and you loathe people as much as you say—then, why have you brought me here?"

He bowed toward her, looking closely to see if she really didn't already know: "You are not like them."

"What do you mean?" She furled into a sitting position. "I'm a human being. The kind of animal you hate."

"You are different." He crawled to her side and curled up alongside her. "Why do you think I came for you? I've watched you grow up. I've seen you step out of your clothes when you thought you were alone in the woods. I've watched you talk to birds and dance—at home in the natural world. I knew you would not be afraid of us or scorn us. And when my chance to have you came—I took you."

She placed a kindly hand on his sun-streaked mane. "I can't stay here with you."

"Why not?" He swung his head into her lap and pouted up at her. "Didn't you have a good time last night?"

"It was—" She almost said 'a dream.' "It was wonderful. I've never felt so free—so vivid."

"You belong with us, Flannery." His hand stroked her cheek and the sinuous length of her white neck. "You mustn't return to the ugly, polluted world of people. You belong here with the Theena Shee in a life between animal and human. In the better of those two worlds."

"Even if this is just a dream," she confessed with a faint flicker of pity in her voice, "even if this is just a fantasy of my concussion, I want to stay here with you. But first, I have to see Neddie again."

"Why?" He rocked his head petulantly. "She won't give you her blessing."

"I know." Her cool fingers brushed the breeze-tousled locks of hair from his brow. "But I owe her everything. She took care of me when I lost my parents. I can't just disappear—not even into a dream."

"Yes, you can." He sat up, jaw set. "People disappear all the time."

"No." She insisted. "I want to see her again."

"Then, see her. Look—" Arden knelt over the clattering brook and with both hands smoothed the ruffled water to a slick mirror. In its reflecting surface, the image of the blond biker faded to a burnished vision of Nedra standing beside a hospital bed, her hands on the rail crusty as the knuckles of an apple tree. Flannery beheld herself in the bed, wan and slack-faced.

"No, Arden." She slapped the water and shattered the mirror to a splash. "I want to really see her—visit her, talk with her."

Arden sat back and tipped his head to one side, appraising the merit of her demand. "Have you forgotten the black dog?"

She chewed her lip, considering this. "I just need a few minutes."

"It's dangerous," he warned. "If the black dog gets you, you die. You lose all this." He motioned to the cloud castles and the sun-filled meadow bobbling with butterflies. "And I lose you."

"You said I had a choice." Flannery pushed to her feet. "Well, let me make that choice." She sloshed across the brook toward the glinting motorcycle. "Take me back."

Arden heaved a sigh and stood up. "It's your life." He climbed onto a wide bough beside the brook and cat-stepped across it to the other side.

Flannery watched him inquisitively. "It's true then?"

He pounced onto the grass beside her. "What?"

"The Theena Shee can't cross through water."

He rocked his jaw thoughtfully but said nothing. Then, he strode past her toward the shining bike. Without looking back, he commanded irritably, "So, let's go."

2.
ZIP TO DO WITH LOVE

To love is to bring forth from yourself what is beautiful.
—Diotima

Nedra, as Flannery had perceived her in the water mirror, stood beside her unconscious granddaughter. The witch's old hands clutched the bed railing with a white-knuckled grip as she stared fiercely across the bed at Chet. The young man had not been visible in the vision, because he had backed out of the scene, retreating toward the door.

"You leave this room," Nedra growled, "you kill her."

Chet stopped. "Don't say that."

"Would she be here now if not for you?" Her leathery hand brushed Flannery's long hair, a gentle gesture full of the serenity of her despair.

"It was an accident."

"And only you can undo it." The wrinkles between the witch's eyes smoothed and the lynx tufts of her eyebrows lifted hopefully. "Will you?"

"How? How can I undo this?" Chet stepped toward the bed, staring piteously at Flannery. "The doctor says she's dying."

"She *will* die unless you save her."

"How am I supposed to save her?" He studied Flannery's dreamless features with blinking bewilderment. "What do you want me to do?"

Nedra's opalescent eyes brightened, full of joy and sadness, both at once. "Do you know where I live—where Flannery lives?"

"The curio stand on Old Mill Road."

"You go there tonight," she ordered, her breath blistered with urgency. "At midnight."

"I can't go there at midnight." Chet snorted with disbelief. "My parents . . . "

"Don't tell your parents," Nedra demanded. "Don't tell anyone. You go there tonight at midnight, and we will work the Fetch."

"The Fetch?" Chet swallowed and looked away, toward the door and the world of sanity. "You've said that before. What's that? Magic?"

"Flannery's only hope." Nedra leaned over the bed toward Chet, her hands on the side rail, trembling. "You must go after her into the Otherworld and bring her back."

"The Otherworld?" Chet looked stricken. "What are you talking about?"

"You knocked her soul out of her body," the witch grumbled. "Trying to get away from you, she lost her soul. The Theena Shee have her now—and they will not let her go. You must fetch her. You must convince her it's worth coming back."

"Mrs. Fell—" Fear tinkled along his spine as he contemplated the consequences of enraging this crazy hag. He didn't want her showing up for dinner again. "I don't know anything about souls or the Otherworld or the Theena Shee, whoever they are. I can't help Flannery. I'm just a high school kid."

"Chester, you love her." She spoke tenderly. "I heard you say so. I've read your poem. With that love, you can bring her back."

"The kind of magic you're talking about—" Chet shook his head, his lens-enlarged eyes liquid with emotion—"I don't know the first thing about it."

"I do." The crone stepped sprightly around the bed. "I am a Wiccan priestess. I can send you to the Otherworld. Come to me tonight at midnight, and I will show you where Flannery is—and how to fetch her soul."

"I don't know, Mrs. Fell . . . "

"Call me Nedra." Her merry smile squeezed light from between her prune-skin eyelids. "We will be working closely together—and for a soul we both love."

Chet nodded to humor the crone and heard his neck creak with tension. He walked to the door and stopped to stare at the aged patient sleeping in the first bed. The sight of her surrounded by balloons, sprays of flowers, and a jumble of get-well cards pinched his heart for Flannery, who had nothing but the love of a balmy grandmother. He slid a leery look toward the witch. "Is this *really* going to work?"

Her blue stare burned into him. "Do you *really* love her?"

Chet answered with a worried frown and got out of there.

3.
TRICKED OUT GHOST

The soul's faithfulness to this world is the ghost.
—Madame Blavatsky

The flowers on the aged patient's bedside dresser shivered, and their slender vases began clinking together and then rattling and clacking loudly. The bulletin board trembled and shook, its frame knocking against the wall, get-well cards dropping like autumn leaves. Soon, the whole room vibrated with a pneumatic rumble that set dresser drawers banging, chairs walking, and glucose drip bags swinging. Startled by the quake, the old patient stirred from her sleep and sat up.

The bellowing engine noise of a motorcycle stomped aggressively into the room, then coughed to abrupt silence. Arden strode through the door, snakeskin boots thwacking the linoleum, beaded trousers and fetish charms clattering. He turned his radiant smile on the old peach-haired patient sitting up in bed, and she gasped before his pierced visage and naked torso tattooed in blue runes. "Sleep," he breathed, and she collapsed backward into a profound slumber.

The curtain partition flew open, and Nedra Fell stood glowering at the apparition of a pagan biker with lion-colored, windblown hair. "Where is Flannery?"

"Behind me." Arden swept his dark-visored gaze around the room. "I came first to make sure she's safe."

"You dare bring her *here*?" Nedra's wrinkled face clenched with outrage. "In this place, Death will sniff her out in an eye blink."

"She insisted." One side of his mouth turned up with happy impertinence. "She wants to say goodbye, grandma."

Nedra peered past the tattooed shoulder and called meekly, "Flannery?"

A sparkling reply came from the hallway, "Neddie!"

"Child, get away from here now!"

Arden sat in the chair beside Flannery's bed, bemused at Nedra's dismay. "You better show yourself quickly, Flannery. We don't have all day."

Flannery, dressed as she had been at the time of her accident, entered the room and stopped short when she saw herself lying in bed unconscious. Apprehensively, she looked to Nedra. "Neddie, I'm here. Can you see me?"

Nedra gawked at her, horrified. "The glamour! Oh, Flower Face, you have the glamour on you." With agitated hands, the witch opened the bed stand drawer and took out a small mirror. She breathed a hurried chant onto it, then shakily held it up to the wraith of Flannery.

The girl stared stunned at the lucent green eyes reflecting back at her. The angular beauty of her face shone with a pallor of moonlight. She gasped and touched her hair—curvaceous locks, fiery as dusk. "Neddie! I'm beautiful."

"Listen to me, Flannery." Nedra mouth's opened and closed soundlessly like she had difficulty breathing, and her eyes buzzed with alarm. Finally, she said in a gust, "The Theena Shee will destroy you. You must come back."

"Neddie, I'm not coming back," the girl proclaimed triumphantly. "I'm here to say goodbye. I'm going to stay with Arden."

"No, no—he's charmed you, child!" She expelled a sharp, alarmed hiss between her yellow teeth. "The Theena Shee will feed you to the dragon."

Arden clucked his tongue mirthfully. "Didn't I tell you? The old witch doesn't want you with us."

"Neddie, it's not what you think." Flannery gazed affectionately into her grandmother's face that, on the verge of tears, looked even more like crinkled paper. "It's gorgeous where I am. And I'm happy. For the first time in my life, I feel I belong."

"Oh, Flower Face, no." Her thick hands reached out and touched the chill, electric brightness where Flannery stood. "You belong here in this world."

Arden guffawed. "So you can grow old and die among all the many people who love you?"

"Don't listen to him." Tears brimmed in Nedra's eyes. "I tell you . . . "

A ravenous snarl jarred the room.

Arden leaped up and seized Flannery's arm, pulling her toward the door. "Come, quickly!"

Nedra grabbed for Flannery. "She stays!"

"She will die," Arden gnashed.

"Better she die here," Nedra grunted, swiping futilely at Flannery's ghost. "Better she die than suffer what you will do to her in the Otherworld."

"Be gone, witch!" Arden swiftly wrapped the partition curtain around Nedra and fled through the door with a frightened Flannery in tow.

Nedra struggled free of the curtain and whipped it aside.

The black dog came at her, fangs blurred.

"*Dagda Huh-loo!*" the startled witch cried in Gaelic.

The growling beast leaped, and Nedra yanked the curtain about it. Tangled in the fabric, the dog writhed and expanded to a hominid-shape with grasping arms.

Nedra reached behind the bed stand and pulled out the femur wand. She whacked the snarling figure on the head, and the sheet collapsed flat. When she snapped the curtain open, the black dog was gone.

A nurse occupied the doorway. "Is there a dog in here?" She arched her eyebrows disapprovingly. "Pets are not allowed in the hospital."

4.
COOL AS IN STRANGE

Next to God, there is no greater power than knowledge.
—The Mabinogion

Chet sat for hours in the refrigerated chill of the main library. Volumes of mythology, Celtic lore and magic entombed him in his carrel. Atop them all, he'd propped open a book revealing an old woodcut of Orpheus leading Eurydice up from the Underworld. For him, this confirmed that indeed there was a hallowed tradition for what Flannery's psychowitch grandmother wanted him to do. That didn't mean she wasn't crazy, just crazy in a way people had been for a long time.

After eating his lunch of cashew stuffed sweet potato balls and vegetable cake in the library courtyard, he continued his research at a computer console. The monitor scrolled images of fairies with bodies tiny and luminous as dandelion seeds, mischievous pixies like four-year-olds with pointy ears, and an assortment of solemn wizards, wrathful witches, and elves with handsome eyes—all of them, to Chet, simply ludicrous caricatures satirizing human vanity.

He read with mounting incredulity the accompanying texts, shaking his head at all this hooey. Yet, he couldn't pull himself away from the phantasmagoria of walking dead, talking trees, and hollowed hills full of wily trolls and ravishing frost maidens—until a librarian coolly informed him that he'd exhausted his allotted time in cyberspace.

Before relinquishing the keyboard, he printed a passage about a weird name the crazy old witch had used and that he had found in his research spelled very differently from how it sounded:

Daoine Sidhe (Thee-NAH Shee): literally, 'people of
the mound,' the divine folk of Celtic lore, who departed earth with the coming of civilization; they dwell in
the Annwn (Ah-NOON), the Otherworld, a parallel di-
mension, whence they come and go freely, taking what
shapes they will.

Chet departed the library and biked to *A Moon for the Myth Begotten*,
an occult bookstore in the sullen precincts of town. Often from the school
bus, he had glimpsed the peculiar building that housed the store, its pink
minarets and blue mosaic façade winking past from a narrow cobbled lane
between a dingy auto parts shop and the industrial barn that housed the
city's snowplows.

In that forlorn alley, on those uneven stone lozenges with their oily ha-
loes, he walked his bicycle, and his heels clattered loudly, inspiring echoes
that lingered ominously in the gloomy lane.

He couldn't guess how this garish bookstore had wound up here between
anonymous depositories of soot-black brick—unless a genie had conjured
its pointy Moroccan doorway and storefront clad in small, square, blue
tiles. The genie must have worked his magic long ago, for many tiles had
chipped or fallen away, leaving whole swatches missing, exposing an un-
dersurface of gray, powdery brick.

Chet leaned his bike against the grimy mosaic and gazed up at a sign
that once portrayed a cratered moon but now, rain-worn and bleached, resembled an anemic pizza encircled by pseudo-Arabic script: *A Moon for the
Myth Begotten*. Oddly enough, high above the hokum minarets and pink
gables of crocketed sandstone embossed with scarabs and sphinxes, a real
moon of nearly transparent silver drifted in the day sky.

Chet needed both hands to open the ponderous black iron door with its
ornate hinges of tangled arabesques. It screeched on those rusty hinges and
shut fast behind him with a resounding dungeon portal boom.

A brisk, resinous scent like Christmas trees embraced him, and he entered a vaulted room of bookshelves crammed with antiquated, leather-
bound volumes. Curved walls, ribbed by granite groins, resembled the
interior of a castle. Instead of tapestries, the walls displayed elaborate as-

trological charts, framed arrays of medieval tarot cards, a Cabalistic 'Tree of Life' busy as a street map, Tibetan mandalas like festive birthday icing, and a poster-size photo of Aleister Crowley, bald, massive, and staring at the viewer with demented fixity.

"Can I help you?" From the stacks emerged a clerk with freckled pate, flaxen goatee, and a lean, Slavic severity remindful of Vladimir Lenin. "Are you looking for something in particular?"

"Uh, yes, actually I am." He knew he'd come to the right place when he noticed that the clerk cradled an open portfolio book of watercolors depicting brownies and sprites wearing flower-petal dresses, acorn caps and cobweb shawls. "I'm looking for information about a Celtic ritual called the Fetch. You heard of it?"

"Yes, I've heard of it." The clerk closed the portfolio with ceremonial care and pressed it against his chest. "May I ask why you want to know?"

"I'm preparing a school report." Telling a lie didn't seem wrong in this sanctuary of fables, lore and esoteric fictions. "I'm writing about Celtic myths. So far, I've been to the library and searched the Internet, but I haven't been able to find much about this ritual."

The bald scholar set down the art book on a sturdy reading table. "As I understand it, the Fetch is not so much a ritual as a journey out of this world and into a magic realm called the Otherworld." His tone did not indicate anything strange, but his narrowed eyes and tucked-in chin suggested the transmission of secret and dangerous knowledge. "It's a wonder journey intended to recover a person abducted by the fairies."

"You have any books about it?"

"Just the usual literature you would have found in the library." He cast a bland look at the encumbered bookshelves. "Poems of Yeats. Some supernatural stories by various Irish and Welsh authors."

"How does it work—this wonder journey?"

"That depends on the story." The clerk's features once again tightened to a conspiratorial squint. "But I can tell you this, very few people who make the journey to the Otherworld come back. The fairies enslave them—or throw them into hell—or sacrifice them to trolls or a dragon." He placed both hands on the table and leaned forward emphatically. "Celtic fairies are *not* like Tinker Bell. To the monks who first heard about them from the druids, they were the fallen of heaven, human-sized, wicked—and very dangerous."

Chet nodded thoughtfully and turned toward the heavy iron door. "Thanks." Squealing like an instrument of torture, the exit relented to his push.

"If you want more information," the clerk called after him helpfully, "there's an old woman, a Wiccan priestess, who sells pagan fetishes and Celtic curios out on Old Mill Road . . . "

5.
WICKED WICCA

For love's bitter mystery, a man will wander long beneath the disheveled stars and even dare to enter hell.
—Robin of Connaught

Lena had prepared a dinner of apple-beet-blue cheese salad, bisque of chanterelles, and grilled Thai sea bass with portobello compote—a meal complex enough to keep her worried mind occupied during her trying day.

"The school called," Elliot informed his son, helping himself to a peanut-crusted, basil-laced wedge of steaming fish. "You skipped today."

"I was at the library," Chet answered nonchalantly but kept his gaze on the festive meal before him, not wanting to look at the garbled blue-and-yellow bruise on his father's brow. "I did a lot of reading."

"You could have told us, Chester." His mother delivered a piqued stare. "I was worried after what happened last night. It was all I could do not to call the police and tell them that addled old woman had abducted you. And if you hadn't come home by dinner, I would have."

Chet picked at his salad with his fork, segregating chunks of apple, beet and blue cheese. "I needed a day off—after yesterday."

"We know it was a terrible shock for you," Lena allowed, trying to sound less angry. "What happened to your classmate is traumatic."

"And we think maybe a counselor might be of help." Elliot packed his mouth with a twist of Choctaw carrot bread, aware of the implication that inhered in that statement—the unspoken question of sanity. "You know, someone who understands how to deal with tragedy."

"That way you can talk with an expert about your feelings," Lena quickly elucidated.

"I think that's a good idea," Chet readily agreed, to the obvious astonishment of both his parents. "I've been thinking the same thing. It's time I see an expert."

Such full and willing compliance allayed all concerns at the dinner table, and from that point, the meal progressed with the usual light-hearted banter about local sports, the antics of a neighbor's pygmy pig, and news from an uncle in Umbria. Neither parent thought to pursue just yet which expert Chet would consult, and they would have fallen out of their chairs had they known what he had in mind.

Their ignorance permitted them to slip into deep, restful sleep in the day's final hour—while Chet dressed for a vigorous outing: hiking shoes, jeans, plaid shirt, and baseball cap. The digital clock on his bed stand read: 11:37 when he made his final decision to go to Nedra Fell and consult with her. Perhaps some technique beyond the purview of medical science could save the comatose teen. Somewhere he had read that harp music sometimes roused coma victims.

He stuffed pillows under the covers of his bed, opened the bedroom window and crawled out. Descending the wisteria trellis at the side of the carport, he landed gently among mimosa shrubs.

Chet pedaled with alacrity down the middle of the empty streets. Awash in the cold radiance of mercury-vapor streetlamps, he made swift progress on his flight from town. But once he left the paved streets and turned onto the dirt road that would eventually take him to *Nedra's Celtic Curios & Pagan Fetishes*, he rode more cautiously, afraid of losing his balance on the rutted surface illuminated only by the pewter light from the setting moon.

Insects chirruped and an owl hooted above the swish of his tires. Ahead, a mammoth human silhouette reared against the night sky. Limned in moonlight, the giant Woman Made of Flowers loomed into view.

Chet's bicycle glided to the roadside stand, where shining gourd lanterns hung from the eaves. He dismounted and left his bike lying in the grassy verge beside the souvenir stand's twig-framed sign. With trepidation, he confronted the many fleshy-faced poppets dangling between the beaming lanterns.

"Nedra?" he called out uneasily. "Nedra Fell? It's me, Chet."

He peeked about anxiously and then cautiously walked into the road-side stand. Among the skeletal shadows of rattles, walking staves, shields and drums, many withered apple faces watched.

"Nedra—are you in here?"

A drum throbbed deep as thunder, rattles sizzled like vipers and a crackling shadow abruptly lurched toward him. He gasped and backed into a stack of staves, knocking them over with a startling clatter.

A face swung into the amber glow of a gourd lantern, a face brown as a crumpled bag. "You're late!"

"Nedra!" Chet huffed with relief. "You scared me."

"I dozed off." The crone blinked wearily. "You were supposed to be here at midnight. It's almost one."

"It was farther than I thought."

"Never mind." She shook her head, looking faintly disgusted. "You're here now. There's still time. But we must move quickly. Take off your clothes."

"What?" he quacked, startled. "Why?"

"During the Fetch, you will need protection from the Theena Shee—the spirits who have abducted Flannery." The witch stared at him hard-eyed. "The best way to deflect their weapons is to turn your clothes inside-out."

"Weapons?" Doubt about his coming here in the middle of the night pounded like an ache in the hollow of his chest. "What kind of weapons?"

"Bone knives." A predatory scowl grooved the old woman's features. "Whittled ribs of their victims. Quite sharp, yet they can't penetrate the inverted clothing of the living. Do be careful to protect your hands and face, though."

"Wait a minute." Chet stiffened. "We have to talk."

"There is no time!" the witch snapped. "At this moment, Flannery is being seduced by Arden, prince of the Theena Shee. You must hurry!"

"Hold on. Wait up here." Repelled by the hag's fanatic urgency, Chet backed away and knocked over a drum, producing a stunning boom. He jumped and waved his hands about in a dither. "I thought we were going to conduct a séance or something. You know, fetch Flannery's soul back with our love for her. Maybe some chanting."

"No, you fool." Nedra grabbed him by the arm and started unbuttoning his shirt. "You have to go *get* her!"

"Get her?" He pushed her away and stumbled clumsily, toppling shields and more drums. "Where? Where do I have to go to get her?"

"I didn't call you here for schooling," the woman growled. "Moments are precious now. We must act and act quickly. Do you want to save Flannery or not?"

"Of course I want to save her," he replied in a gallant but small voice. "Why do you think I came?"

"Then, you must trust me." Nedra's words glinted with a special hardness. "I will not lie to you, Chester Hubert. What you are about to undertake is perilous. You may die."

"Hey!" A jet of absolute terror shot up his spine. "I don't know about this."

"You consulted Doctor Antone." She spoke severely. "You know Flannery will be dead in a few hours. I'm telling you—only you can save her. But you must risk your own life." The crone lifted her cleft chin. "Do you love her enough to do that?"

"To *die*?" he asked with delirious force. "Oh, God, I don't know . . . "

"Then, you better go home," the witch declared flatly. "The Fetch is not for those who doubt or fear for themselves. Go home, Chester Hubert."

"Look, I'm sorry." Chet eagerly stepped away, gingerly avoiding the drums and shields he toppled. "I didn't know it would be this dangerous."

"What did you think?" Nedra flared snidely. "Flannery's life is at stake. She is in the hands of creatures willing to kill for her. She cannot be saved by a séance—or a *poem*." She recited his poetry with squeaky derision, "'Come back. If you die my life is a lie.' Bah!" She added bitterly, "She *is* going to die. And no words can stop that. Only life can defeat death." With a rueful shake of her head, the crone turned her back on the timid boy. "Go home, Chester Hubert. Go home and forget about Flannery Lake. For the sanctity of your own soul, forget you ever thought you loved her."

Chet stood perfectly still, quivering inside, buffeted by the old woman's harsh words. Reaching deep into himself, he asked, "What do I have to do?"

Nedra faced about with a stubborn slowness. "Trust me." A disdainful sweep of her rheumy eyes appraised Chet. The old eyes locked on his, daring him to look away. When he managed to hold her gaze, she told him, "Never doubt me. Or your life is forfeit."

Wariness veiled his stare. "Just tell me what I have to do."

"Take off your clothes."

Chet drew a long breath and quickly stripped all his clothes except his eyeglasses. The shame of cowardice that she had stirred in him defeated all embarrassment, and he stood unflinchingly naked before the old woman.

"Leave your underwear off," she instructed. "Nothing comes between your flesh and your protection. Turn your clothes inside-out and put them back on."

Chet obeyed, inverting his jeans and stepping into them, then his socks. He pulled his shirt inside-out, put it on and fumbled with the buttons.

"I know this seems impossible to you, what we are doing." Nedra's thick fingers nimbly helped him button his shirt. "How can clothes turned inside-out protect you from knives?" She smiled kindly. "You will be contending against spirit powers. Their forms seem the same. So human. So familiar. But the rules are different. Magic rules where you are going."

Chet frowned. "But I don't know where I'm going."

"Your ignorance itself will be a weapon." She patted his shoulder impatiently. "Put your boots on."

Chet stepped into his hiking boots, knelt and laced them.

"You are a warrior now." Nedra spoke in an incantatory cadence. "A spirit warrior. You are Flannery's champion." She turned his cap inside-out and placed it firmly on his head. "She will not be expecting you to come for her. So, when you find her, it will be your task to win her."

"How?" Chet finished lacing his boots and stood, heart brimming with worry. "How will I win her?"

"With your love!" Her eyes caught the vague illumination from the gourd lanterns in blue carats, as if ice packed her bony sockets. "With your love—and with the truth."

Chet's heart squeezed, and doubt tightened within him. "But what is the truth?"

"The truth is that Arden and the Theena Shee have no love for Flannery." The diamond bits of her stare bored into him. "They want her dead. They have stolen her from this world to sacrifice her to the dragon."

The cinch of doubt around his heart constricted with painful incredulity. "There really *is* a dragon? Like in the storybooks?" He felt like a hopeless idiot in his inverted clothes, miles from anywhere, long after midnight, and listening to this madwoman speaking to him about dragons.

"Yes, of course there is a dragon!" She yanked back her head, marveling at his ignorance, appalled and pitying. "It is a magnetic beast. It lives inside the planet. It is quite real—and very hungry for souls. If the Theena Shee do not feed it, it will devour them."

Chet's Adam's apple rose and fell. "Am I supposed to kill it?"

"No." She emitted a dead laugh. "It *cannot* be defeated. This is not a fairy tale dragon, Chester. This is a planetary monster as old as the earth itself. But don't be afraid." She gripped both his shoulders and squeezed them as if imparting courage. "It's unlikely you will face it, for it lives deep underground. It is the Theena Shee you must fear. They will fight you for Flannery."

As much to humor her as sate his curiosity, he inquired, "How do I fight them?"

"It will go better for you if you don't." From a capacious pocket of her sack dress, she withdrew a necklace of marble-sized brown beads—hazelnuts, he realized, as she placed them over his head and around his neck. "So long as you wear this, you are invisible to the Theena Shee."

Chet fingered the hazelnuts and wondered if next the old bird was going to outfit him with a helmet of aluminum foil so the spirits wouldn't read his thoughts. "These are hazelnuts."

"*Magic* hazelnuts." She chucked him under the chin with her callus-bossed knuckles. "Trust me."

As if out of the moon-glossy air, she plucked a palm-sized Celtic cross of iron and held it up before his surprised face. "If you need to defend yourself, use this. It is made of magnetic iron and will burn with mortal pain any of the Theena Shee it touches." She pressed the Celtic cross into his hand.

Chet examined it quizzically, fingering the medallion for runes or other magical engravings and feeling only smooth metal. Then, he met Nedra's penetrating stare.

"You feel like a buffoon, don't you?" She smiled with almost childish zeal. "Standing here with your clothes turned around, wearing a necklace of nuts, and talking to a loony hag about spirit powers and a dragon." Her crinkled face offered a nod of grandmotherly sympathy. "Come. I will end all your doubts."

Nedra and Chet exited the souvenir stand, Chet walking stiffly as he crammed his hand into his inside-out jeans to put the Celtic cross in his pocket. The witch led him down the moon-paved road toward the Woman Made of Flowers.

"There is no way to prepare you for what you are about to experience," she rasped with excitement at Chet's impending discovery. "You must simply enter the Otherworld. When you arrive there, you will know the truth of it."

"How will I find Flannery?" Chet asked, contributing his full rational attention to the old woman's fantasy. "And what do I say to her when I find her?"

"Listen for the music," she answered with a daft directness. "Follow the music. The Theena Shee are wooing Flannery. And when you find her, talk from your heart. Make her listen. Her life depends on it."

At the Woman Made of Flowers, Nedra reached among the blossoms and pulled open a section of the wicker scaffolding.

"What is this thing?" he asked, peering up at the giantess posing seductively before the starry night.

"This is the Woman Made of Flowers," the witch answered with hushed reverence. "Blud-eye-eth."

"Who?" Staring at the alluring figure against the splatter of stars, he experienced a touch of vertigo as if suddenly caught in a massive wave lifting him higher into the smoldering darkness.

"Blud-eye-eth is a fabled woman of Celtic myth." The witch's eyes shone in the dark like tiny silver mirrors. "The name means 'Flower Face,' which is the owl's poetic nickname, the bird who steals souls—for Blud-eye-eth was a woman made from magic and flowers and, like the owl, she had no soul of her own."

The myth invoked something in him like a touch of destiny. "Why is she here?"

"Magic," Nedra replied, showing all her many crooked teeth. "Everything here is magic."

6.
PIT OF DARKNESS

Upon that road hammered silver by the moon go the proud and the careless to the Otherworld.
—**Thomas Traherne, *Elucidations of a Severed Head***

Chet poked his head into the entry to the Woman Made of Flowers and saw pencil-thin rays of moonlight piercing the interior and touching stacks of peat bricks, a shallow depression cut into the earth, and a root-cellar door with a rope handle.

"In you go." Nedra took him by the wrist and guided him forward, her spider-silk hair glowing like a radioactive cloud in the dark. She led him to the edge of the depression, which opened before him with the unfortunate size and shape of a shallow grave. "This is the gateway." She stepped down and yanked open the root-cellar door by its rope handle, revealing a pit of absolute blackness.

"Down there?" Chet gawked into the grave dark.

"It's okay, Chester." She turned her withered face toward him, her eyes all pupil. "There are no rats or spiders in there."

"I'm reassured." He approached and sat down on the brink of the opening. "So, you want me to go in there, huh?"

In the deep shadows of the enclosure, the witch's face seemed expressionless, yet her voice punched him, "Hurry! Dawdling only endangers Flannery."

Chet winced and lowered himself, reaching with his foot for something solid. He touched soft ground, cushy as moss, and eased himself down. Only the top of his head remained in the sketchy light, and he looked up at Nedra anxiously. "There's nothing in here."

The crone whipped him with a command, "Lie down!"

Chet obeyed and disappeared in the darkness.

Quickly, Nedra closed the door then stood atop it and securely knotted the rope handle to a latch on the jamb.

"Hey!" Chet's muffled voice called out. "I can't see anything!"

Nedra walked out of the ankle-deep depression, and the door behind her juddered, pushed from within. Methodically, she began tossing peat bricks into the cut earth, and they thudded dully atop the shuddering door.

"Open up!" Chet demanded. "Nedra, open the door! I can't breathe! Hey! I'm getting dizzy."

As Nedra continued heaving loamy bricks onto the door, Chet's muted cries grew dimmer and more infrequent and eventually succumbed to silence.

Within the unremitting darkness of the pit, Chet breathed heavily, his heart thudding louder in his chest than the peat bricks falling atop the door. He berated himself for the stupidity that had led him to such a miserable death. He had not prayed since he was a little boy, and his mind fumbled in a panic to recall supplications from childhood. "Oh, God! Oh, God!" he babbled when all he could remember was grace.

A spark of light glimmered in the total darkness, and initially he assumed it was a retinal flare from his bulging eyeballs. But then it brightened to a star, and his heart thumped more furiously, suspecting that this *was* God or the notorious tunnel of light on the way to the afterlife.

Gradually, the star widened to the serene disk of a full moon. A mentholated breeze caressed him, carrying a fragrance of spruce woods.

With an astonished cry, Chet jumped to his feet and dementedly confronted a forest slashed with moonlight. Insects chirred, and an owl sobbed repeatedly.

"Nedra!" His shout folded into echoes through the raggedy trees. Insects and the owl fell silent. Far off, he heard a throbbing pulse of music.

He rubbed his face with both hands, then peered once more into the forest of silver moonbeams. "Am I dreaming?"

He kicked a tree hard, and the impact jarred his leg painfully. "Ow! Damn it." He hopped on one foot. "Get a grip, Chet."

He angled his head and turned about, listening past the loud beating of his heart. "Nedra said music would lead me to Flannery," he mumbled to himself, needing the sound of his own voice to steady his nerves.

An instant ago, he had been lying in a shallow grave, and now he stood staring at bearded trees rooted in fog like pools of swirling milk. This frontal assault on reality compelled him to do something, anything to preserve his sanity, and he stalked off into the phantasmal forest.

7.
MAULER'S DANCE

Who would fight devils but for love?
—Huth Merlin

Chet moved cautiously through luminous woods. As the pulsating music grew louder, he jogged more swiftly down moon-bright lanes of mossy trees. Ahead, he glimpsed violently dancing figures and quickened his pace.

His breathing scooped deep into his lungs, stamina wearing thin. The driving rockbeat of the music masked his gasping approach.

Close enough to see the sweaty faces of the dancers, faces full of impish mischief, he stopped. His cap had fallen off during his run, and his dark hair, loosened from its combed restraint, dangled across his eyeglasses. He brushed back those obscuring strands and stood with his hand grasping his head, astounded, watching the animal frenzy of the dancing Theena Shee.

Bestial eyes streaked like sparks. Hair bristled thick as fur over naked shoulders—and fangs rayed in their laughing mouths.

Chet backed away, frightened. Then, he spotted Flannery in the slamming crowd, dancing ferociously with Arden before a colossal disfigured oak. She looked more beautiful than he'd remembered, her hair extravagant fire, her face haughty as a highland princess.

Drawn to her, he entered the moony air of the glade and the raucous din of music. Like a shackled man, he plodded past couples of Theena Shee grappling amorously among trees immersed in fog vaporous as ether. Eyes fixed on Flannery, he wended amid crazed, pelvic dancers.

The Theena Shee danced around him with undiminished vigor, oblivious to his presence. Invisible, he made his way closer to Flannery through the churning dance mob. The press of the manic throng jostled him, and the hand of a gyrating dancer snagged the hazelnut necklace. Nuts flew like buckshot, ricocheting off surrounding dancers.

An unearthly shriek pierced the revelry, and the pounding music fell silent. The Theena Shee crouched and glared at Chet avid as wolves.

Chet screamed, "Flannery!"

Flushed with exertion, Flannery spun about in time to see Chet seized by the Theena Shee and dragged kicking out of the glade.

Bone knives flashed in the moonlight and stabbed Chet. The blades clacked off his inverted clothes as if rebuffed by armor.

Covering his face with his arms, Chet shoved through the enclosing Theena Shee. Their angry shouts lashed him, and he bolted into the forest. With outraged howls, they pursued. An infuriated gang of shadows in the moon smoke, they flurried among the trees.

Chet fled for his life, arms pumping, feet high stepping over roots and rocks. He wove among the trees, heart punching, legs hollow with fear.

A pack of predators, the Theena Shee swarmed closer, eyeglints stripes of fire in the dark, screeches and brutal cries ripping the night.

Chet stumbled and rolled down an embankment in a vortex of churning leaves. At the bottom, he scrambled to his feet, panting in terror, and splashed across a creek. He tripped over a fallen bough and sprawled to his back on the far side, face smeared with fright, hands uplifted to ward off his rabid pursuers.

The Theena Shee stopped cold on the other side of the creek. Arrayed along the bank in a tangled mass, they hissed and droned with frustration. The sparks of their beast eyes flared hotter.

Whimpering, Chet rolled to his feet and sprinted into the dark tunnels of the forest.

8.
DEVIANT

Children the witches steal to molest before Satan,
who drinks of their blood.
—Maleus Malefiarium (The Hammer of the Witches)

"Ches-ter!" Elliot knocked softly two times on his son's bedroom door, tapping in rhythm to the syllables of his name. "Mother's already called you to breakfast twice. Get up, lazybones." He gave the doorknob a flick and a gentle push. "You're going to be late for school, son."

Elliot approached the bed, turned back the covers and, when he saw the pillows packed to resemble a sleeper, let out a mournful moan. "Lena—get in the car!"

The bat-winged bruise on his forehead throbbing with indignation, Elliot knew exactly where to drive. The Huberts' blue compact pulled up with a rasp of gravel in front of *Nedra's Celtic Curios & Pagan Fetishes* and jerked to a sharp stop. Elliot flew out the driver's side, slamming the door.

Lena, still in her floral housecoat, emerged from the passenger seat and left her door open. "Maybe we should call the hospital again."

"Why?" Elliot grumbled. "Third time's a charm? He didn't go to see the girl last night. He has to be here."

Lena stood on the shoulder of the road staring at the Woman Made of Flowers, then, with disquiet, at the rickety stand festooned with pagan artifacts. Her dour gaze floated across the rowdy yard inhabited by disfigured stone gnomes to the overgrown and rusty trailer home. "Why would he come here?"

"That witch stormed into our house the other night to prey on his guilt." Elliot strode around the car toward the roadside stand. "He came here to appease her. I know it."

"Chester!" Lena called shrilly.

"Look!" Elliot dredged Chet's bicycle from the high, feathery grass beside the twig-framed sign.

Lena wailed, "Chester! Where are you?"

Dropping the bike, Elliot hurried into the souvenir stand. A moment later, he yelped, "My God!"

"What?" Lena stood paralyzed beside the flowery giantess, her whole body leaning forward from the ankles, impatient to know what her husband had found and yet afraid to see. "What is it?"

"Get out your cell." Elliot stepped forth from the decayed souvenir stand holding Chester's underwear. "Call the police."

9.
SHINING MOMENT

Faeries covered in moss and the flower—
Upon green sods await the moth-hour.
—Sir William Rufus, *Under the Bell-Branch*

Flannery sat beside Arden between a gnarled tree and the burbling brook that traversed the meadow of wild strawberry, rhododendron and everlasting. Spellbound music floated half-heard along evanescent eddies of dandelion fuzz and drifts of sun-dust. The Theena Shee lay scattered in comfort on tussocks of sphagnum moss and bracken, butterflies looping around them, while overhead bales of cumulus tumbled in slow motion.

"Chester Hubert—" Flannery shook her head in wonder. "I never thought I'd see him here."

"Aren't you sleepy?" Arden mumbled, arms-crossed behind his head, resting on a bed of lavender asters. "Rest. Save your strength for night."

"What happened to him?" Flannery inquired, her tone implying he had suffered a dire fate.

"I've already told you," the prince of the Theena Shee muttered under breath. "He ran away."

"You wouldn't lie to me?"

"I have no reason to lie to you," he said with a soft smile and an ingenuous shake of his head. "We're happy together, you and I, aren't we?"

"I've never been happier, Arden. I just never expected to see him here."

"Nedra sent him." He spoke with somniferous gentleness. "Who better to call you back to the drab world than the very one who drove you out of it?"

"But how did Neddie talk him into coming?" She pondered this with a frown, still convinced this was a dream yet expecting some kind of logical consistency from her trance. "I can't imagine him having anything to do with magic."

From a sleepy distance, Arden said, "Nedra can be very convincing."

"She was never able to convince me any of this was real." Flannery released an elongated sigh and surveyed again the lustrous meadow, her gaze returning to rest on her drowsy companion and the cinnamon glint of his downy cheeks. "It took you to do that."

"Then, you'll stay with me?" Arden rolled to his side, dark glasses mirroring her pallid face and floating hair. "You don't want to go back?"

"Go back to what?" She screwed up her eyes and bit her lip. "To school? To making curios with Neddie?" She tossed her hair back defiantly. "There's nothing there for me. All my happiness is here—with you."

She stretched out beside him and hugged him. Together, they cuddled under the charm of sun-dust, tumbling clouds, and dreamsprung music.

86

PART TWO

KILLING WITH THE
EDGE OF THE MOON

The moon leaks dreams into the awful darkness of
the world. These lost dreams look to mortal eyes like
starshine, stellar smoke, the Milky Way. The barge
of the dead finds its path by that light across the broken waters. In its wake, faerïe gather up the spilled
dreams of the moon with wild pumpkin lanterns.
The shadows that live by that glow cavort upon
the grooved walls of our brains as silhouette pup-
pets—lust and terror jerked awake by faerïe strings.
Who are the faerïe? They play the human heart like a
harp. If we hear their music on the thin roads of the
wind, we must not listen. If we listen, we slip out of
ourselves and down the roads of the wind into their
brighter world, where our shadows die.

INTERLUDE:
WALKING THE BLACK DOG

Trees are doorways to the underworld.
—**Edgar Figge,** *The Alphabet of Trees*

Chet shambled aimlessly through sunny woods. For hours, he had wandered among the forest's primeval chambers, first by moonlight, then under the twisted silk scarves of dawn, and now with daylight drifting through the trees. The whole time, he had been alert to bestial cries on the wind, fearful that the Theena Shee would pounce on him again.

He knew he should rest, even sleep if he could find a covert where he felt safe, yet he experienced no fatigue. His body felt light as smoke—far lighter than his mind, which burdened him with questions: What was this place of giant, mossy trees and aromatic humus? Who were the Theena Shee, those animals disguised as people? And why was he here in the first place? Did he actually expect to rescue Flannery? She didn't look like she needed rescuing: she had looked happy—*wildly* happy—dancing with the Theena Shee. Nedra had said he had to win her back to the human world with his love. But by what magic did he hope to inspire her to love him? He might as well try to impress her by plucking sunbeams for a bouquet or taking down the moon for a charm.

A gentle wind soughed across the forest canopy glittering with bird chirps and whistles. He stopped in his tracks. From down a corridor of pines, a muscular black dog watched him. He returned the bitch's stare.

"Come here, girl." He whistled softly. "Come here."

The large black dog approached slowly.

"That's a good dog." Chet bent down and extended his hand for the animal. "Come on."

The dog stopped just out of reach.

"You live around here?" he queried with good cheer, glad to meet another mammal in these desolate woods. "You know where I am? I've been walking for hours, dog. I'm lost. I'm cold. And I'm hungry."

The massive canine watched him fixedly with eyes of crushed diamonds.

"You don't look cold or hungry," Chet noted with comradely concern. "Any idea where the hell I am?"

The black dog turned and strolled away, then paused to look back.

"Sure." Chet straightened tiredly. "Why not?"

The black dog walked with strong purpose down the avenue of pines, and Chet trailed after.

The pines eventually thinned to a grove of spindle trees threaded with sunlight. Chet struggled to keep up with the large, spirited animal. Weird how fatigue came and went in this magic forest like a distant memory easily forgotten. He fell behind, and the dog had to stop and wait for him to catch up. "Don't look at me like that," he beefed the first time, when he still had breath to talk. "This is the most hiking I've done—ever."

In a dark tunnel of large, pitch-green trees, a regal white elk crossed their path, regarded them serenely and bounded away. Deeper in that dark temple of huge trees, mists unscrolled. The dog continued onward, leading Chet to where no direct sunlight squeaked through the high canopy.

Mist thickened to knee-high fog, and Chet shoved into a jungle of ferns. An owl sobbed dolorously.

He followed the dog till they came to a bleak clearing enclosed by black ferns and spectral willows. The underbrush crouched in dimly primate shapes. At the glade's center, a hospital bed floated on a carpet of fluorescent fog. Flannery's comatose body lay in the bed flanked by drip bag and monitor—and Nedra Fell stood alongside.

The black dog showed her fangs and growled.

"Shh, girl." Chet bent and stroked the beast's ruff while grinning with relief to see the witch. "It's all right. These are my friends. Good dog. Good girl."

Nedra's eyes widened, horrified. "Why did you bring *that* here?"

"What?" Chet stood, perplexed. "The dog? It brought me here." His head slouched forward. "What are *you* doing here? I thought you couldn't enter the Otherworld."

"Do I look like I'm in the Otherworld?" The witch glared at him grouchily and rattled the bed railing. "Flannery is dying, Chester. That's why the black dog led you here." Her skull sockets leaked blackness like two holes punched in a mask. "You must act quickly!"

"I tried." Chet waded through fog, past the snarling black dog. "But the necklace broke. The Theena Shee almost killed me! They're animals!"

Nedra jutted her jaw impatiently. "Try again."

"But I'm not invisible anymore."

"Whose fault is that?" She shooed him away with both rugged hands. "Follow the music, Chester. It will take you to the glen where you found Flannery before. And this time, move quickly. Go directly to the giant oak. There is a door in its trunk. Pull it open."

"How will that help?"

"That door leads to the dragon grotto." She fixed Chet with a knowing look of cunning and defiance. "Open it and the blast from within may shock Flannery back to her senses."

"*May?*" Chet croaked.

"It's a risk." The crone stuck out her lower lip and hunched her shoulders. "You may both die."

"Oh, at least we got that straight." Chet rubbed the weariness from his brow. "All I wanted was to go to the spring dance with her—and now we're already at death do us part."

An enraged bark erupted from the black dog.

"Go now!" the witch insisted, skittering sideways like a spooked cat. "At once—or there is no hope." Her already scowling visage tightened meaner. "And get that dog out of here."

TAKING DOWN
THE MOON

Through the ashes and wreckage of sunset, the
dragon peers out of a fiery abyss into our dim world,
searching for human prey, for those who wander
alone at the bottom of the day.

1.
BUTT KICK THE CRONE

What parent is not a lion in defense of the child?
—Ben Jonson

Elliot stalked angrily into Flannery's hospital room followed by a fretful Lena. They glanced at the elderly woman with the peach-colored hair lying in the bed closest to the door. She looked up from the dog-grooming magazine she was lazily thumbing and smiled benignly.

With a huff, Elliot strode past her, and Lena nodded a cursory greeting.

"Where is our son?" Elliot demanded of Nedra Fell, who remained seated beside her granddaughter's bed. He ignored the unconscious girl, his stern gaze fixed on the crone.

Lena went directly to the bed rail and poured attentive concern over Flannery.

Nedra offered Elliot a placid look.

"Please," Lena appealed with one hand on Flannery's cuffed arm, testifying as a mother, "if you know anything, tell us."

Nedra nodded sympathetically to Lena. "Chester is in the Otherworld."

Lena's hand flew to her mouth, knuckling back a gasp.

"What do you mean?" Elliot's jaw throbbed. "He's dead?"

"I hope not." Her seamed face expressed genuine worry. "He has gone to the Otherworld to fetch Flannery's soul."

"What are you talking about?" He tipped his head backward, assessing the sanity of the old woman. "Where has Chester gone?"

"Chester loves Flannery." Nedra reported this as a solemn fact. "If anyone can bring her back, he can."

KILLING WITH THE EDGE OF THE MOON

"Bring her back?" Elliot's eyebrows knotted a flummoxed frown. "Your granddaughter is right here. Where is our son?"

Lena gently placed a restraining hand on her husband's arm and tried to explain, "Mrs. Fell, we found Chester's bicycle and—and his *underwear*—at your place. You must know where he is."

"I've told you," she insisted with beneficent calm. "Chester is in the Otherworld. I know that is difficult for you to believe. But it is the truth."

Elliot lurched forward, grabbed Nedra by her hempen gown and gruffly lifted her to her feet. "Listen, you old witch, you're going to tell us where Chester is or I'm going to shake the teeth out of your head!"

"Elliot!" Lena pulled at her husband's arm, vainly trying to break his hold on the startled old woman.

While they struggled, a nurse rushed in, shouting, "What is going on here? You! Let go of her!"

Lena danced hysterically beside her husband. "Elliot—please!"

With a strangulated cry, he released Nedra, and she plopped down in her chair stunned. "You're insane!" he accused in a hot whisper.

"Leave the room at once," the nurse directed, jabbing a finger toward the door and rushing to Nedra. Covering the old woman in a human shield, she glared over her shoulder at Elliot. "Get out now."

Lena hooked her elbow through her husband's taut arm and drew him backward toward the door.

"We're going to the police." Elliot spoke quietly, his voice uninflected with the fury that pulsed in the green vein squirming down the middle of his bruised forehead. "You hear me?"

The woman with the peach-colored hair slid down in her bed, hectically flipping glossy pages of coiffed poodles and blow-dried sheep dogs.

95

2.
THERE IS A DRAGON TO FEED

The Otherworld is the dragon's world.
—The Daoine Sidhe

Beneath their gnarled tree beside the murmuring brook, Arden slept and Flannery lay awake in his arms. She carefully disengaged from his embrace, stood, and looked around at her sunny surroundings. The Theena Shee slumbered among flowery hummocks of the meadow and on the rootweave of the enclosing forest. Fine, bright filaments of forest fluff floated on the beryl breezes.

She strolled through the grassy selvage of the brook, and basking toads hopped away in every direction. Kneeling among cobbles emerald with moss, she smoothed the chuckling water with both hands. For a moment or two, she admired her own reflection in the mirror-slick surface. Then, she intoned, "Show me Chester Hubert."

A crisp vision appeared in the water, revealing Chet stumbling through a misty grove of willows.

"How did you know how to find him?" a drowsy voice inquired.

Flannery startled and lifted a guilty smile to Arden. "I imitated what I saw you do."

On a rock speckled with lichen, he sat beside her. "At least now you know I didn't lie about Chester. That's your fear, isn't it? That all of this is a lie?"

Flannery ducked behind the red veil of her hair. "The Theena Shee *are* famous for tricking people."

His yellow, creaturely eyes peered at her from above dark glasses. "I would not deceive you."

"There is a dragon to feed," she answered, flicking her hair back with an emphatic toss of her head.

"Ah, the dragon again." He thumbed the sunglasses up the bridge of his nose. "Yes, it must be fed. And what choice do we have?" His cheeks puffed out and deflated helplessly. "It was here first, you know. We didn't always live in this world. Once we dwelled upon the land where cities and highways flourish now like canker sores."

"Yeah, yeah—none of you wanted to live in a world of walls and breathe soot," said Flannery, tagging on with her eyes 'I know.'

"So, we took refuge here in the Otherworld—the dragon's world." Sadness pinned his eyebrows higher on his forehead. "If we are to survive here, the dragon must be fed. Small price to pay for all this beauty and rapture, don't you think?"

"Is that what you're going to do with Chester?" she asked frankly. "Feed him to the dragon?"

"I told you." He tenderly brushed a strand of hair from her eyes. "We steal away people no one misses, people who have already abandoned their lives. Lost souls. They die swiftly. Painlessly."

"Chester is not a lost soul." A twinge of pity flickered in her at the thought of geeky Chester thinking he could trespass the Otherworld and save her. "He has parents who love him."

"If we catch him, we'll throw him back into the city from whence he came." Arden got off his perch and knelt beside her. "Do you believe me?"

"I want to."

"But this is all so new, you're nervous, aren't you?" He packed his voice with mock worry. "You have butterflies in your stomach. Here. Let me help." He patted her back hard.

With an amazed expression, Flannery clutched her throat, and when she opened her mouth, out popped a butterfly!

Arden laughed with childish glee as it fluttered away, and he slapped her back again. Another butterfly unfolded from her mouth. This time, she giggled as it unfurled bright wings and lofted away. Surprised, she threw her arms around Arden as yet a third butterfly blossomed from her open mouth.

Soon, the air about the laughing couple swarmed with the flickering confetti colors of a dozen jostling butterflies.

3.
A CLASSIC VIEW OF HELL

The way into hell is easier to find than the way out.
—Faust

The black dog trotted among dense trees raddled with mist, and Chet loped after it, struggling to keep up, breath rasping. Sunlight pale as milk seeped through latticed leaves of crooked cottonwoods, mossy hickories and oaks dangling ivy and grapevines. Crickets trilled, and a crow cawed.

"Hey, slow down," Chet gasped as the dog disappeared into one of the forest's dark alleys. "Damn!" He stopped, put hands on knees and caught his breath. "Maybe 'damn' isn't the best expletive for where I am right now." He drew a long breath. "How about—'nuts!' Nuts! I wish I had those hazelnuts." He straightened and glanced about timidly at the impressively ancient and dark forest. "I wouldn't mind being invisible here." Pushing his eyeglasses more firmly in place, he surged on into the dismal woods.

Hours later, with a huge moon rubbing against black spires of pine and fir, crickets buzzing, and yet another owl sobbing, he ambled wearily into a clearing and paused. Distant music vibrated on the wind.

He continued profiled in smoky moonshafts, following the music past somber yews and the mournful whistle of nightbirds. At a stand of white birch feathered in mist, the concussive, speed-metal rhythms grew louder. He saw, bracketed by the skeletal trees, Flannery and Arden aglow with un-earthly beauty embracing in a dance of fluid, loose and erotic abandon.

The Theena Shee had all paired up. Their bodies interlocked in whip-ping dervish whirls and sensuous blurs of ecstasy.

Chet clenched his fists. The lenses of his eyeglasses glared over with sil-ver moonfire reflecting from the glade. He knew what he had to do, but he was afraid. The tendons in his neck tightened as he coiled his strength, and his tired knees wobbled. With a hopeless cry, he burst out of the dark niche of trees and into the shining clearing.

Running with grim determination, he darted among the dancers. He nailed his focus on Flannery and saw nothing but her body lewdly intertwined with Arden's. When the astonished Theena Shee cried out and tried to snatch him, he shoved past them.

Shouts of alarm flared like feral howls. Brutish eyes flashed with malevolence. Clawing hands grasped for Chet, ripped his shirt and sent him stumbling to the ground. The Theena Shee hurled themselves atop him, yelling and snarling. The frenzied music crashed to brawling noise.

Then, shrieks of pain cut through the murderous cacophony, and the Theena Shee hurtled away, flung into the air and rolling across the ground in motion blurs of agony. Chet lurched upright, the Celtic cross in his hand wisping with fleshsmoke.

Flannery, in Arden's arms, peered blearily at Chet. "Chester?"

The Theena Shee stepped back as Chet strode among them, flashing the Celtic cross like a detective's badge for all to see. "Flannery—get away from him," Chet warned, flushed and breathless. "He's the Devil."

"Is that what the witch told you to say?" Arden asked through a tight smile. "I'm the Devil now?"

Chet took hold of Flannery's arm and pulled her away from Arden. "We're getting out of here," he told her, his cheeks and neck feverishly blotched but his bespectacled eyes remarkably amber and calm. "I'm taking you back home."

"I'm not going anywhere with you, Chester." Flannery wrestled free of him. "What are you doing here?"

"The witch sent him." Arden inched closer, and Chet drove him back with the Celtic cross. "Nedra knows you will die in her world if you don't go back tonight." Arden pointed a questioning look at her. "Do you want to go back, Flannery? Do you want to wake from your coma and live in the ugly world?"

"No," she replied instantly. "I'm staying here with you." She swung toward Chet a look vibrant as an electric current. "You shouldn't have come. I'm happy here with the Theena Shee. I'm happy for the first time in my life."

"Flannery, this is all some kind of weird dream." He waved his arms broadly at the towering trees weaving the moonlight into laser beams that reflected off the creaturely eyes of the seething Theena Shee. "In the real world, you're *dying*. You want to die?"

"Yes, Chester," she agreed with sour resignation, "I want to die in that stupid world. I don't want to live in my body anymore. I want to stay here and live as a spirit being." Her eyebrows arched sharply. "Clear enough for you?"

"I don't believe you." He seized her arm again. "You're under their spell."

She shook him off like something filthy. "Go home, Chester."

"Live with it, Chester," Arden gloated. "She wants me."

"She doesn't know you." Wild-eyed, Chet searched the handsome face behind the dark glasses. "You're not even human."

"You're right." Arden reached out with dazzling speed and snared Chet's wrist, twisting it until he dropped the Celtic cross. "You have no notion how happy I am to be Theena Shee and not one of your stinking breed."

Grimacing in pain, wrist pressed to his chest, Chet whimpered, "If we stink so much, why do you want her?"

Arden motioned to the Theena Shee. "Get him out of here."

Chet locked an urgent stare on Flannery, heartened to see her green eyes widen with alarm as the Theena Shee clasped his arms.

"Don't hurt him!"

"Wait!" Chet scuffled frantically. "Let me say goodbye. Flannery, please." His hands reached out desperately, spidering the air for her. "I came all this way. Let me say goodbye."

Flannery fired a haunted look at Arden, whose upper lip curled back with unmasked contempt for the boy. "Arden," she entreated, touched by Chet's desperation, "give him a moment before you send him back."

Arden reluctantly nodded for his gang to release Chet. "Be quick about it."

Chet threw off the bruising hands of the Theena Shee and stepped close to Flannery, speaking with tremulous fright, "Nedra told me to talk from my heart when I found you." He squeezed her hand, his eyes moist, as much from the pain in his wrist as from the hopeless care he felt for her. "But you don't really want to hear that from me. I'm nobody to you. And that's okay. I guess the truth is I didn't come here for you."

He spoke in a rapid, emotional patter, all the while stepping gradually sideways until the huge, distorted oak stood at his back and Flannery came between him and Arden. "It's my fault your body is lying in a hospital bed right now—dying. I can't live with that. So, what I'm doing now, I'm doing for me. I want to do this. I want you to know that. I'm doing this for me. So, don't feel bad later. I'm taking responsibility, because I got you in this trouble. That's all it is. Okay?"

Flannery regarded him coolly. "Chester, what are you talking about?"

"It's time to go, Chester." Arden aimed a blind, ruthless smile at Chet. "Say farewell."

"Farewell, Flannery." He sprang to the giant oak, grabbed hold of its rough bark and pulled with all his might.

A collective gasp expanded among the Theena Shee, and they rushed forward. Flannery watched, baffled, until Arden dragged her away. "He's mad!" he cried with fierce despair cold rage. "The witch crazed him!"

A massive door in the trunk of the oak groaned open. Crimson rays lanced from the widening portal, and an eerie sizzling spit like voltage. With a momentum of its own, the titanic door swept Arden and the Theena Shee aside. Chet fell to his haunches, and ichorous red light poured over him revealing a pulsating fiery interior.

Within the open gateway of the gargantuan oak stewed a torrid subterranean vista, a classic view of hell—crumbling ledges of brimstone, black slag and sawtoothed lava stepping downward in obscure terraces. At the bottom ranged a dry lakebed, caked slurry cracked through to a molten core hissing sulfur steam and blue jets of flame. The acetylene brilliance illuminated clotted arches and stalactite lofts of a gruesome cathedral.

Embedded in the obscene convolutions of lava stone squatted dozens of people, abducted victims of the Theena Shee, their twisted bodies trapped like insects in gobs of amber glass drooled with lavish epoxy mania over grasping limbs and anguished faces. The chorus of their stifled howlings moaned like a tempest wind.

Up from this steaming, cauterized pit, imps flurried—demonic versions of the Theena Shee, blunt-faced as vipers, grinning evilly, long mouths full

101

of teeth, warty flesh flapping like leather, eyes fiery puncture holes—minions of the dragon. Gibbering and screeching, the goblins plucked up Chet and hauled him swiftly into the infernal deeps.

The goliath door swung shut with such force the reverberating crash lifted Flannery off her feet. She flew backward, hitting the ground hard, and darkness glared over her.

4.
JAGGED MORNING

The sleeper wakes, yet the dream remains.
—**Gregory Walsinghame, *Fallen Fruit***

A wrenching sensation jerked through Flannery. She opened her eyes to a fluorescence white as the inside of a refrigerator. She was lying on her back in bed. Arden, the Theena Shee, Chet and the hellish vision of screaming people had dropped away like a renegade dream.

Her vision focused, and she saw, leaning over her, Nedra, kindly eyes glistening with tears. "Neddie?"

"You've come back whole." Nedra's aged features beamed. "You are a lucky one, Flower Face. A very luck one."

The squalor of Flannery's nightmare persisted. "What happened to me?"

"You don't remember?"

"I was hit by a bus." Words burned her parched throat. The frightful vision of hell together with the rapturous memory of the colorful meadow floated eerily in her mind, a mirage atop the darkness of the universe, adrift in the blackness that had possessed her when the bus struck. "I saw myself. I saw myself—lying on the ground. And then—and then I had this crazy dream . . . "

"A dream—yes." Nedra's cracked leather face bobbed in agreement. "A crazy dream."

Flannery became aware of the drip tube in her arm and plucked at the adhesive tape securing it.

"Wait, child." Nedra placed a restraining hand over her granddaughter's impatient fingers. "Wait for the nurse."

Other than her dry throat, Flannery knew no pain. "I feel fine." She snapped off the tape and sat up. "I don't need this." Sleep and dreams vanished before the miraculous world of the waking. She extracted the drip tube, feeling strong and clear-headed.

"We're in a hospital, Flannery." The old woman groped for the nurse-call button. "We should consult the doctor."

Flannery threw off her bed sheet. She touched her legs, her knees, her toes. The solidity of her body was the shape of her fate. Bizarre dreams, the memory of the bus striking her, and the opinions of doctors dribbled away before the actuality of her flexing hands.

She lowered the side railing and sat on the edge of the bed, facing the bulletin board, empty except for Chet's poem, written in precise block letters:

> If you die
> my life is a lie.
> Come back.

A sharp knock on the open door diverted her attention to a large-boned, platinum-haired woman in crisp, professional attire. "Nedra Fell?" From a small, black utility bag, she produced a gold badge. "I'm detective Mowbray."

5.
OUT OF SIGHT

The world we see is not the world that is.
—Nedra Fell

Squad cars with rooflights flashing jammed the shoulder of the dirt road beside *Nedra's Celtic Curios & Pagan Fetishes.* Their red shadows battered the night forest, flickering against the stark trees like ghostly fire. Headlights basked the Woman Made of Flowers, and searchlights mounted on the car doors cast brilliant beams across the weedy yard and its minions of stone gnomes onto the vine-entangled trailer home. The loud bleat of police band radios seemed to make the stars rattle.

Officers with flashlights searched the roadside stand and surrounding grounds. Their shadows swarmed hugely over the yard. Inside the flowery giantess, detective Mowbray stood beside a high intensity tripod light watching two uniformed officers remove the last bricks of peat from atop the root-cellar door.

When they finished, they stood aside, and the large, platinum-haired detective snapped on a pair of latex gloves, stepped in and untied the knotted rope handle. She swung open the cellar door, flooding the pit with light and exposing packed earth and a few tendrils of looping roots.

6.
EVIL STROKES

Those lost in the Otherworld peer back into this world with faces like
mirrors, and the residents of earth see them not.
—Seamus O'Boyne, *Enchantment in the Hollow Hills*

Chet squinted upward into the blinding radiance of the high intensity tripod light. He discerned the silhouettes of two cops and a bulky woman
gazing down at him. Distantly, he heard the woman announce, "Nothing
here. It's empty."

The shadows of the cops shrugged, and the large woman closed the
root-cellar door, smothering Chet in darkness.

Derisive cackling sounded nearby, the source invisible in his momentary blindness. Jolly gasps and gaggling grew louder, and as vision winced
back, gruesomely warty faces of snickering imps hovered into view. They
leered at Chet with cankered lips and orange eyes.

Horrified, he saw that he lay on his back in an infernal grotto of fluted
stalagmites rust-red and glossy as raw meat. Gabbling, caterwauling goblins surrounded him, poking him with crooked sticks, and his arms and
legs flailed, trying to protect himself.

A blister-lipped imp plucked off Chet's eyeglasses and, jabbering with
glee, smashed them onto the cancerous face of another hob. This inspired
a renewed frenzy among the fiends, whose gnarled sticks thwacked Chet in
a savage tumult. He bounced with each blow, and his anguished cries com-
peted strenuously with the wrawling laughter of hobgoblins.

7.
COLD REVELATION

Know thyself.
—The Delphic Oracle

Amidst the mess left by the previous night's police search, Flannery rummaged angrily. She brusquely pulled aside bales of dried herbs, knotted masses of twine, sheets of bark and an overturned stool.

Nedra watched tranquilly from where she sat at the kitchen table sipping a cup of tea.

"That was no crazy dream that happened to me," said Flannery with a surly glance at her grandmother. "It was real. I *was* in the Otherworld. And I saw Chester there."

The old woman inhaled the spicy aroma of the brew with flaring nostrils and hooded eyes. "If you say so."

"If I say so?" Flannery rose from her haphazard search and stood with hands on hips. "For years you've been telling me about the Theena Shee and the Otherworld."

"And for years you've said none of that was real," Nedra countered complacently. "It was just a story."

"Neddie—" Flannery slogged through drifts of corn silk intended for poppet's hair. "Last night, detective Mowbray said Chester's bicycle and *underwear* had been found here. It was enough for a search warrant. Why won't you admit what happened?"

Nedra's eyebrow tufts lifted a notch. "What did happen, Flower Face?"

"You sent Chester after me," Flannery said, voice alight now with indignation. "You told him where to find me. You told him about the door in the oak."

"Maybe it was all just a dream." Nedra sipped her tea.

"It was real." Flannery stepped over fallen poppets to reach the table of varnished maple. "Everything you've told me since I was a child is real. I know that now." She leaned over Nedra, frowning. "Don't deny it."

The witch met her frown with a quiet stare. "Sit down."

"I want to know where Chester is."

"Please." Nedra motioned to the empty chair beside her. "Sit."

Flannery begrudgingly sat and said in a pitch of fear that rose to a whine, "Neddie, I saw him dragged into the tree—into *hell*!"

Nedra stopped her by placing a gentle hand on her arm. "Listen to what I have to say, Flower Face." The witch returned her tea cup to its saucer and appraised her granddaughter with stony pride. "You know now that I have told you the truth all along. I am not the mad old woman you thought I was. I am a Wiccan priestess of an ancient lineage, and I know whereof I speak. So, listen very carefully to me."

Her grandmother held Flannery with a stare furiously calm as a hawk's, and the young woman's heart surged, simultaneously thrilled and terrified of the truths about to be revealed.

Nedra continued softly, "The morning you found me unconscious atop my altar in the forest and you thought I was dead, I very nearly was. I had worked a ritual meant to buy me more time in this world."

"The black dog *is* Death." Flannery acknowledged this with a shiver. "You tried to thwart Death."

"Yes, Flower Face." Nedra sighed desolately, and Flannery saw behind the shine of tears a velvet darkness of bad luck in the old woman's pupils. "I tried to thwart Death, and I failed. I wasn't strong enough to complete the ritual. And instead of winning more years of life for myself, I unleashed the black dog—and she went after you."

Flannery sat back under the weight of this disclosure. "That's why the bus hit me."

"The bus hit you because you didn't look where you were going." Nedra sneered with disapproval, then her critical stare blurred. "But once your soul was knocked free of your body, Death made her claim on you."

"Arden saved me." Flannery spoke in a hush. "He got me away from Death and took me for himself."

"Arden never wanted you for himself." The disapproving sneer returned with vigor. "He took you for the dragon."

"But he—"

"Made you happy. I know." Her prune-skin eyelids fluttered with disbelief at her granddaughter's gullibility. "Arden was just biding time. Your soul was bound to your body in the hospital. If he had thrown you into the dragon pit, the terror of that experience would have frightened your soul back into your flesh. Which is exactly what happened when Chester opened the door to the dragon grotto."

"Did Chester wake up too?" she asked with lofty hope. "Where is he?"

"No, Chester did not wake up." Nedra lifted her teacup as if to salute his courage. "He was never asleep, you see. I sent him body *and soul into the* Otherworld." She sipped her brew and then added with a pensive sigh, "He belongs now to the dragon."

"No."

"Yes." Nedra set down her cup with the finality of a gavel. "There is nothing you can do about it."

Flannery's shock stretched her stare right through her grandmother. "Chester doesn't deserve to die."

"Who deserves to die?"

"Not Chester." Her head rocked back as if her brain had just swerved to a stop. "He thinks he was responsible for what happened to me. But it was *you*." She tightened her gaze. "It was you set loose the black dog. If anyone deserves to die it's you, not Chester. He's just a kid."

"He is young, yes—and I am old." Nedra admitted this with trancelike composure. "I am very old indeed. Yet I need more time."

"Why?"

"For you, Flower Face," she answered, blinking with surprise that Flannery even had to ask. "For you."

"Don't give me that." Flannery shoved her chair away from the table. "I don't need you."

A cryptic glimmer of sadness shadowed the witch's icy eyes. "You need me more than you know."

"What are you talking about?"

"You have no friends," Nedra said glumly. "You have no interest in school. Or clothes. Or music. Or movies. You're never happy except when you're alone in the garden or the woods." The old woman turned her face and gave her granddaughter an oblique, inquisitive look. "Why do you suppose that is, Flower Face?"

"I like to be alone." Flannery absorbed Nedra's criticism with cross-armed indifference. "So what? That's not important. Chester is in hell right now because of me. *That's* important."

"This is the first time I've seen you excited about another human being." The grandmother appreciated this by rubbing her whiskery chin. "Maybe my ritual worked after all."

"What do you mean?"

"Until now, Flower Face, you've had no heart for the world of people." Nedra spoke in a subdued and savvy tone. "Your soul belonged to nature—and to the Theena Shee. That worried me. That worried me a great deal, because I'd kept you in this world hoping you would discover your humanity. I thought if I bought more time, perhaps I could help you learn what it means to be human."

Her grandmother's words set a harp-string in Flannery's chest twanging discordantly. "What are you saying?"

"Your parents did not die in an automobile accident."

Flannery's face budged forward. "What?"

"Your father was my great-great-great-grandson." She reported this bluntly. "His parents were the ones killed in a highway accident when he was a young child. He came to live with me. I taught him the ancient ways. I was wrong." The anguish of memory deepened the furrows of her brow. "I should have allowed him to live his fated life. But I wanted a blood heir, my own to pass along the ancient knowledge. *Wicca.* What hope of that dream from this old flesh? I thought your father was a divine answer." She compressed her lips ruefully. "He learned well. He was versatile at crossing between the worlds. And in the Otherworld, he fell in love with a woman of the Theena Shee. That was our second grave mistake. The princes of the Theena Shee disapprove of interbreeding. They sacrificed your father and his lover to the dragon."

Flannery nodded hypnotically and surmised in a cold whisper, "But not before they had a child."

"Yes," Nedra said with a tragic smile. "A beautiful baby girl. I hid her all these years. I tried to teach her human ways. I wanted her to be wholly human, because I knew the Theena Shee would destroy her if they found her." Her head bowed sadly. "I wanted her to be human. I tried to buy more time for myself—for her—because I wanted the time to teach her to be human."

This revelation piled through Flannery. It packed her skull with stupefaction and displaced her thoughts, pushing them out through her wide eyes, to evaporate in thin air. From far away, she heard herself asking, "Why didn't you tell me?"

"Tell you what?" the witch asked, a trace of irony in her voice. "That you're only half in this world? I didn't want what happened to your father to happen to you,"

Flannery's thoughts poured back into her head with crushing force: "And so now, a real human being is in hell because of me."

"He sacrificed himself," Nedra avowed soberly.

"You sent him after me." Her accusatory tone kinked into anger and lashed the old woman. "You knew the Theena Shee would take him."

"I explained the risks," she said, head high. "He chose freely. Anyway, why should you care? He is nobody."

"*Nobody?*" Flannery stood, face shrunken, hot and hard. "He's not nobody, Nedra. He's one of the smartest and kindest kids in school—and he has a future." She squared her shoulders. "I'm not leaving him in hell."

"There's nothing you can do." A flimsy wave of the witch's hand dismissed the boy. "He is in the dragon grotto." Her stare crisped. "No one escapes the dragon grotto."

Flannery turned her back on the crone and resumed rummaging through the tossed room. "It would have been better if you had left me with Arden and let him feed me to the dragon."

"I couldn't bear to lose you, Flower Face," she confessed with fugitive sorrow. "What are you looking for?"

Flannery reached under a collapsed stack of willow withes Nedra used to secure animal skins to her drums and came up with the elk thighbone. "A weapon."

"No!" The old woman's afflicted voice vibrated harshly. "Don't talk crazy, girl. If you go back to the Otherworld, you will both die."

"Maybe so." Flannery hefted the femur wand. "But I can't live in this world with Chester dying in the Otherworld." She didn't give Nedra time to reply but strode through the clacking nutshell curtain and into her bedroom.

Many tiny rainbows spun across the bare walls from the prism mobile in the shining window. She tossed the femur wand on the cot and opened her narrow closet. After taking out a white ceremonial gown stitched in runes of parti-colored threads, she began to strip her baggy street clothes.

Nedra watched from the doorway teeming with rainbows. "What are you doing, Flannery?"

"This dress—" She nodded to the lambent and frilly garment as she dropped her pants. "It's the ceremonial gown you made for me to wear on ritual days—Sow-en, Loon-ya-sah, Brigid." A wry laugh squirmed out of her. "I used to think it was just a pretty dress for your so-called holy days. But now I understand—this gown has its own magic, doesn't it?" She answered herself with a knowing nod. "It will protect me in the Otherworld."

"Don't do this, Flower Face." The crone's words staggered from her, heavy with fear. "The Theena Shee will destroy you."

"Maybe I should be destroyed." Flannery stood naked before Nedra, her lily skin painted in jittery spectra. "Have you thought of that? I'm not happy in this world. And I'm not wanted in the Otherworld. Why should I live at all?"

"You're talking nonsense." The pleats of her throat shook with the conviction of her statement. "You have a soul big enough to live in both worlds."

"You should have told me that long ago." Flannery slipped the ceremonial gown over her head, and rainbow chips sparkled off the many tiny mirrors stitched into the runes. For an instant, she seemed woven of light. "I should have known about myself, Nedra."

"Now you know. You are half human and half Theena Shee." The witch leaned into the room. "Stay with me, Flower Face. Stay with me, and I will teach you magic."

"If what you say is true, Neddie, I don't need to learn magic." Flannery stepped into her brogans, picked up the femur wand and lightly nudged Nedra aside. "I *am* magic."

She pushed through the clattering nutshell curtain, hurriedly maneuvered among the chaos of the kitchen and the crafts room, and bolted out the door. Purposefully, she sped across the weedy yard, ignoring Nedra's cry from the doorway, "I'm sorry, Flower Face. I'm sorry."

Nedra's worried frown bent to a small smile as soon as Flannery dipped out of sight behind the Woman Made of Flowers. In her careworn eyes expanded a soft expression of triumph and pride. "I'm sorry I had to push this hard to wake you." She chuckled with exultation. "But now—now you have a heart—and all the pain and danger that go with a heart."

8.
RANSACK THE PIT

Who but a true hero may raid the
underworld and come back alive?
—Ellis Cook, *Celtic Myths*

Flannery sauntered down the middle of the dirt road, sunlight spinning off the mirrors of her ceremonial gown. Emerging from the sun-dappled shadows in the woods on either side of the road, impish, lovely faces of the Theena Shee watched her. Exuberantly, she waved her thick wand at them and called, "Brothers! Sisters! Send my lover to me. Where is my Arden? Where is Arden of the Theena Shee?"

Above, in the billowing cumulus clouds, more elfish expressions observed her.

"Arden!" Flannery cried out. "I know you hear me. If you want me, come for me. I am yours now in body and soul."

A menacing growl drew her attention to the roadside, where the black dog stepped forth, fangs meshed, eyes ablaze.

"You!" She smacked the wand against her palm and stepped toward the snarling predator. "You think I'm afraid of you? You're the easy way out. Beat it."

She brandished the wand, and the black dog backed off, dissolving into the darkness of the forest.

A rumble of engine thunder rolled down the empty road, and from around the bend Arden came riding his bike, sun-bleached mane floating in the slipstream. Flannery returned to the middle of the road and stood in the sudden bluster of wind that preceded the rider, gown pressed tight against her narrow body, hair blown to a red aura.

Arden sped directly toward her, grinning mischievously. At the last moment, the bike canted and pulled to a stop inches away. "Flannery Lake!" He laughed passionately, jolted by her willingness to die. "I was afraid I lost you."

"And I was afraid our time together was a dream." Her russet eyebrows bent with sweet pity. "But now—you're here."

"I'm no dream, Flannery." He jerked a thumb down the road, toward town. "This world of people and their walls, that's the dream. It won't last. But we are forever. We are old as the wind, and we will never die." He offered her his gloved hand. "Come away with me."

Her eyes shed a compelling brightness. "I want you, Arden."

She smacked him hard across the face with the femur wand, knocking him off the bike. He thudded onto the road, rolled in the dust, and sat up, dark glasses ajar, beast eyes crossed in a stupefied glower. He rocked for a moment, straining to see straight, then flopped backward.

Flannery mounted the bike and cast a scornful scowl his way. "I want you—out of my life."

She revved the engine aggressively and peeled away, spewing a cloud of dust that swirled to frowning imp faces.

Out of the dust, Arden rose. He scuffled forward, animal eyes humorless, and a tight, evil obsession in his gritted face.

Once beyond sight of Arden, Flannery left the road. She stowed the femur wand crosswise behind the saddle and rode along a bridle path through the forest's green light. After a while, she slowed to a stop, engine purring, and listened. A tint of fluent music on the wind guided her off the bridle path and along a stony trail.

Mist shoaled among birch trees, trees white as bone. On the far side of that ghostly grove, distant figures flitted. She gunned the engine and drove hard through the trees to a clearing she recognized.

The Theena Shee's glade appeared empty. At the far end hulked the giant oak, its disfigured trunk gored by lightning to a mask of blind sockets, and its upraised roots gaping like a crocodile's maw.

The music she had followed streamed from the goliath door in the oak. The huge portal stood open, cleaving the tree as though the oak were an enormous theatrical set, a stage prop. From within, viscid red energies pulsed like magma.

Flannery heard leaves rustle and twigs crackle behind her. She glanced over her shoulder and sighted the Theena Shee in the depths of the forest. They had lured her into the glade. Now that she had entered their ambush, they emerged, rising from behind mossback logs, through veils of muscadine vines, and around gangrenous old trees festooned with toadstools. Their elfish and quarrelsome countenances wore no dark glasses, their rapacious eyes shining with homicidal purpose.

Emitting a belch of engine noise, Flannery's bike skittered across the glade. Her tires tore the loamy ground, kicking up clots of wet earth as she sped straight through the clearing and into the oak's open door.

She knew that the Theena Shee had swung wide the door to receive her. She was the quarry and the Theena Shee in the underbrush the beaters. They had driven her into their trap.

They thought that.

The speeding bike carried her across a high-domed cavern of dripping stalactites. The arching walls of the immense cave ranged surrealistically larger than the stupendous oak that contained them! Scarlet reflections rippled over the vault, shining wetly on stone fangs and uvular rocks hanging above—and on slag walls, where many mangled bodies dangled, limbs caught in twisted glass, eyes swiveling, mouths moaning.

Flannery tried not to look at the impacted bodies. She revved the engine to stifle the cries of their suffering, and she anchored her attention on the infernal radiance glowing at the far end of the ghastly grotto. There, the cave floor ended abruptly at a chasm that plummeted into percolating lava fires.

"Chester!" Her shout and the grumble of the bike joined the echoes of misery rebounding from the stone scallops and hanging spires. She was afraid to scan the convoluted walls, afraid she would find Chet's mutilated body jammed in among the many tortured victims of the Theena Shee. "Chester!"

She rode the bike in a wide circle around the grotto, daring quick sideglances at the contorted people crushed into the rock walls. Red veils of light wavered over their paralyzed shapes, only their eyes jerking, mouths gaping, fingers flexing and clenching.

"Chester!" she hollered and pulled to a stop at the center of the cavern, engine rumbling.

From behind coral shapes of limestone, figures rose slowly into the blushing lava light. To her left, Chet stepped out of the shadows—eyeglasses missing, hair swept back in raven wings, cheeks hollow, eyes soft and kindled with glamour.

"Flannery—" he called to her plaintively. "You came back for me!"

Then, to her right, another Chet arose, identical to the first. Ahead, several more cloned Chets came forth. Soon, a dozen Chester Huberts surrounded her, each of them handsome with glamour, all clamoring for her attention. "Flannery, get me out of here!"—"Help me! I'm the real Chet!"—"Flannery, no! I'm Chester Hubert. Over here!"

Flannery drowned out their cries with a blast of engine noise. She ran the bike in a tight circle, pushing back Chet and his doubles. Hands grasped, faces beseeched desperately, all blurring as she rolled around faster.

With a frustrated shout, she broke out of the circle and drove to the dragon pit. She stopped at the brink and peered in. Far below, the cracked crater floor oozed bright heat, a fiery mosaic. Fumes seethed to a slithering, knotting shape of breathing incandescence. Serpent-coils unraveled, and a malevolent mask of flame-cored eyes peered up under a brow of swollen lobes crawling with blue lightning. She pulled back sharply.

A dozen pleading Chesters crowded toward her. From behind the saddle, she removed the femur wand and placed it across the handlebars. Then, she pushed off, forcing the gang of look-alikes to jump aside.

She rode back through the cavern, turned around and stood there, gunning her engine, wondering if she was really ready to die. She glimpsed the anguished victims of the Theena Shee buried alive in the rock walls, and the skin of her soul shivered.

"I'd rather be dead," she admitted, knuckles tightening on the handlebars. A deafening peal of explosive pistons and tearing rubber propelled her toward the dragon pit. She flew at the chasm far too fast to brake, and all the Chets pulled back with beaming looks of cruel expectation—except one, who shouted, "Flannery—don't!"

The brink swept toward her, and she leaped from the bike and hit the ground in a tumbling roll, elk thighbone clutched to her body. The motorcycle launched into the dragon pit. Chrome shining gold with lava glow, the machine glided downward, wobbling briefly among thermal veils. Its fuel pod ruptured and ignited, combusting a violent blast that shattered the floor of the crater and ejected a gust of pressurized gases.

An enormous explosion lifted Flannery to her feet. Silhouetted against the fireball flaring from the dragon pit, she seized the lone Chet who had not retreated and ran with him across the grotto. The other fleeing Chets shriveled to imps—and, squealing with fright, darted among the rocky outcroppings, scrambling for the exit.

Goblins bounded out the colossal door followed by Flannery and Chet. Moments later, the deformed oak erupted to a blazing geyser. Gouts of burning bark and spinning tree limbs winged through the clearing, scattering the Theena Shee and pummeling the surrounding trees.

9.
TERRORS OF THE HUNT

Fire, running water and the ebbing tide: against these three,
no faerïe or desolate wraith may prevail.
—Esther Davis, *The Wood of the Horned God*

Among trees that wore scarves of mist, Flannery stopped running. Chet fell to his knees beside her, panting.

"No one's following us," she said, searching back over her shoulder through the somber forest for the eighth time since they had fled the blasted glade. "We got away."

"You sure?" Chet asked, miserably.

"Listen." Birds gabbled in the creaking branches. "No music. We're alone."

Chet sat, propped against a beechnut tree, catching his breath. "You came back. For me."

"Yeah, well—" She blinked at him, abashed. "You went to hell for me."

He bowed his head. "The bus—it was my fault."

"No. It wasn't." She sucked in a long breath. "That was one of Nedra's magic spells that backfired."

"Really?"

"Yeah, really." Flannery sat on a root—shelf beside Chet, the elk thighbone atop her knees. "Sorry you got caught up in all this, Chester."

"Call me Chet."

"I'm glad you're still alive, Chet." She looked him over with an approving nod, barely recognizing him now that faerïe glamour had loosened his hair and those sable strands swerved across an angel's enigmatic face of soft eyes and firm jawline. "It was scary back there. What did those monsters do to you?"

119

"Hit me with sticks." Horror quivered his upper lip, and his dark eyes cringed. "I think they were tenderizing me for the dragon." He held out his arms for inspection. "But look—no bruises."

"It's the glamour—the magic of the Otherworld." She patted his arm with kindly reassurance. "Glamour heals."

"It healed my eyes, too. I don't need my glasses anymore." He brushed back the jet locks of his hair and held her wordlessly in his gentle gaze for a long moment. "And you—you look more beautiful than ever."

She rolled her eyes. "It's just faerïe magic, Chet."

"No." He swallowed hard. "You are beautiful, Flannery. I always thought so."

A frisky breeze blew a nutmeg scent of leaf rot out of the forest, and Flannery pushed herself to her feet. "We better get moving—see if we can find our way out before dark."

Chet stood and shuffled nervously. "If we get out—I mean, when we get out—you think you might go to the dance with me?"

Flannery threw him an amazed look. "The dance?" She laughed coolly and shook her head with disbelief. "After going to hell together, I suppose we can handle the spring dance."

They took bearings by the sun and plotted a course through the woodlands that they imagined would bring them out onto the country road near Flannery's home. But their course lost itself in a maze of leaning hickories, steep-banked brooks and random sinkholes with rainwater at their bottoms shimmering like quicksilver.

"How can we be lost?" Chet complained. "Nedra said this was a spirit world. The rules are supposed to be different here. Magic is supposed to work. So, why isn't it working?"

"Magic is working," she said with odd tenderness given that the oak-moss hanging above their heads could shred apart at any instant and drop a fetid gang of winged monkeys to spirit them away. "The Otherworld is like a dream—if I've understood what Nedra's been trying to teach me. This world has its own logic, and what we think, what we believe, what we feel all have a lot to do with what we experience."

"So, we're lost because we're feeling confused?" The sun slid behind the underbrush distressingly fast. "Can't we just calm down, make our confusion go away, and find the road out of here?"

"Maybe if we stop talking," she said in a gentle tone, "we'll calm down."

Conversation fell away after that, and they proceeded in silence. The physical exhaustion that should have stymied them never troubled their wandering, graced as they were by glamour. Confusion and mental weariness, however, bore down heavily. By nightfall, they bit off curses at each new obstacle in the tumultuous forest.

Crickets vibrated and nightbirds tolled in woodland byways frosted with moonlight. "You sure this is the way out?" Chet groused yet again.

"I'm not sure of anything," Flannery uttered irritably. "This is as new to me as it is to you."

"But Nedra's your grandmother," Chet whined. "Didn't you learn anything from her?"

"I never paid any attention." She hooked her fingers in his collar and pulled him back from the edge of a steep ditch shrouded by honeysuckle. "But you better pay attention where you're stepping. I don't want to find out if the glamour can heal a broken leg."

Begrudgingly, Chet grumbled his thanks and scanned the surroundings more carefully. "Why didn't you listen to Nedra?"

"It all sounded like fairy tales to me." She led the way around the cut, through fumes of fog. "Would you have believed her if she was your grandma?"

"No, I guess not," Chet conceded, trying to imagine Nedra with snakeskin pouches of queer herbs helping his mom in the kitchen or squatting in the living room with his dad scrutinizing the games on TV and offering halftime prognostications with clicking fetish bones. "It is weird, isn't it? I mean, this Otherworld. Where are we really? If this is a tangible reality parallel to our own world, why hasn't science already discovered it?"

She took his hand and guided him up a natural stairway of shale slabs. "Maybe they don't know where to look."

"Or how." Chet gesticulated at the black trees sieving moondust. "This world could be out of phase with ours. The laws of physics seem to apply here and yet . . . "

"Shhh!" Flannery stopped abruptly.

"Oh, yeah, I know." Chet bit his lip and looked at his companion with trepidation. "I'm being a nerd again, aren't I?"

"Listen—"

Melancholy strains of an iridescent music curled with the wind.

"It's them!" Chet's eyes jangled in their sockets, trying to look in every direction at once. "The Theena Shee!"

Flannery grabbed his arm and pulled him into a run. "Come on!"

"But where are we going?"

"Away from the music." She towed him toward higher ground, toward slopes of heather floating like lavender mist in the moonlight. "Quickly!"

"No—wait!" Chet dragged her to a stop and scrutinized the moon-shadowed woods. Below them, he recognized a colonnade of pitch-green trees. The black dog had led him among those trunks thick as pillars, and there a white elk had appeared and disappeared like a vision. "I was here before," he announced excitedly and added in a rush, "I met Nedra in a marsh nearby. You were there, too—in your hospital bed. Maybe that marsh is a gateway between the two worlds."

"Which way?"

Chet pointed in the direction of the dolorous music.

"Are you sure?" She backed away behind a hostile gaze. "That will take us right to the Theena Shee."

"We have to move fast." He reached out and took hold of her wrist. "Let's go!" Chet led Flannery along, and they descended the rough terrain in a run.

Among the lightless nooks of the forest, beast eyes glinted, eagerly watching their prey approach. As soon as Chet and Flannery sprinted into the grove where the watchers waited, the music quickened to the cadence of a hunt. The Theena Shee leaped from the dark tunnels of the woods into the cold light of the moon, yipping and whistling. They had lost their beauty entirely and wore animal aspects: ape-brows, leopard rosettes, satyr horns and flicking lizard tongues.

Chet and Flannery flung wild stares around them, and Chet stumbled and toppled to the ground. The Theena Shee fell on him with ferocious braying. As they tore at him, Flannery lurched about, femur wand swinging, and drove them back.

She hauled Chet upright, and the two bolted, the Theena Shee charging after. Through silky mist, the couple sprinted, hurtling across clearings of brilliant moonlight and plunging again into mottled darkness.

Underfoot, water splattered. A brook shimmered like jelly, and the riffle and purl of its hurrying current washed away the hot yells of the pursuers. Only angry grunts remained—and a loud clacking.

Across the stream, Flannery and Chet turned and saw the Theena Shee swiftly piling rocks into the water, building a dam. The terrified teens leaped about and rushed into the night.

KILLING WITH THE EDGE OF THE MOON

In modern times, the Moon has become a rock. In the time of the faerïe, she was the swollen belly of mother night authoring souls and dreams. Rock and dream. The edge between these realities is sharp— and the faerïe use that edge to kill.

1.
DEMENTED HOPE

Midnight, an old house and within—the witch.
—Gwyn Calliste, Witchcraft: *A Play of Shadows*

In the pearly haze of a clearing, a thatch-roofed cottage crouched beneath a vastly huge moon. Hearth-light shone in the round windows, and smoke seeped from the crooked chimney like a wraith.

Flannery and Chet approached through the forest's bedraggled mist. Chet, his clothes in rags, apprehensively stared about at the hazy darkness, and Flannery knocked on the slat wood door.

At once, the door whined open, and Nedra swiftly ushered them into the cottage.

Chet threw himself on the witch, bawling, "Nedra—get us out of here!"

The crone wheeled with him into a cluttered space: Hundreds of apple-faced dolls hung from the rafters, the wicker-woven walls crowded with tree bark masks. Only one piece of furniture occupied the narrow enclosure—Nedra's tree stump altar displaying hare-skull goblet, black glass knife, and seashell plate piled high with the yellow teeth of carnivores. Lit by a raging fire in a crude stone hearth, the room glowed amber and crimson as twilight.

Nedra pried herself loose from panicky Chet and waved anxiously at her granddaughter. "Close the door, Flower Face."

Flannery secured the latch.

"How do we get out?" Chet hopped like a zoo-monkey. "What do we do?"

With two outstretched arms, Nedra distanced him. "Calm down, Chester."

"Get us out of here and I'll calm down."

126

"There is no way out from here." The witch motioned at the rustic surroundings and the tree stump of magical gear. "This is not an exit or even a sanctuary."

"Neddie—the Theena Shee are right behind us!" Flannery's flushed face buckled, ready to burst into tears. "They'll be here any . . . "

Violent pounding shook the flimsy door.

"Flannery—" Nedra beckoned with a careless voice, as though merely requesting a cup of tea. "Bring me the wand."

Gnashing cries and eerie howls raged outside, and the wicker walls shuddered, toppling masks and swaying the hanging poppets.

"You're a witch!" Chet wailed. "Can't you do something?"

Nedra laid the femur wand atop the altar. The knife of black glass spun rapidly, knocking over the goblet and the seashell, scattering teeth like pieces of candy. "By the stars above!" Nedra stood back, hands fluttering over her grizzled head. "You have taken this wand into the dragon grotto?"

"It was with me when the grotto exploded," Flannery explained, hurrying up behind her grandmother.

"Exploded?" Nedra jumped about with a dismayed look. "You *destroyed* the dragon oak?"

Flannery nodded, drawing a sharp breath through widened nostrils. "It was the only way to get Chet out."

"Oh, children!" Nedra's withered face blanched. "You are in peril."

"Is that your professional opinion?" Chet hunched over as the shrieking intensified and poppets shook loose and fell around them, thudding on the tamped earth with sickening plops. "Do something!"

Nedra plucked the thighbone off the altar and pressed it into Flannery's hands. "This wand has absorbed enormous dragon power." Her jowls quivered with awe. "If you can get it out of the Otherworld, the Theena Shee can never assail you again. But if you leave it here, if you should lose it . . . " More masks and poppets fell, and the cottage shook on its foundation. The witch wrung her bulbous hands. "If you lose the wand—you die."

As if touched with an electric prod, Chet jumped. "How do we get out?"

"Look for city lights." Nedra stabbed a crooked finger at one of the tiny round windows, where enraged simian faces with flameblown eyes swung past, mad to find a way in. "You can see the skyline from here if you get to high ground. Run for the city. I will buy you some time."

"We can't escape the Theena Shee!" Flannery yelled above the din of screeches and yowls. "They're too fast—and they always know where we are. We can't hide from them."

"They smell Chester." Nedra glanced at Chet, and her face quaked as if on the brink of psychiatric collapse. "Your ritual gown masks your scent, but they smell him."

"We'll split up," Chet offered, afraid the witch was considering throwing him to the Theena Shee to fulfill her promise of purchasing time for her granddaughter. "I'll lead them away."

"No." Flannery grasped his shoulders. "I came for you. I'm leaving with you. We go together." She shot a glance at her grandmother. "You, too, Neddie."

"I'm not *here*, child," Nedra announced with incredulity at Flannery's assumption. "This is only my double. They can't hurt me." She retrieved one of the fallen masks and set it ablaze at the hearth. Scurrying to the exit, she lifted the latch, and the door banged open. "Now, go!" she yelled, swinging the burning mask at the screeching Theena Shee, driving them back.

Flannery and Chet followed timidly as Nedra led them out of the cottage. The witch, hooting with pyromaniacal laughter, swiped the fiery mask at the surging and shrieking Theena Shee, pushing them aside and opening an escape for the teenagers. "Run!" she squawked. "To the city! Run, children!"

Flannery and Chet bolted for the woods. As the Theena Shee rallied to pursue them, Nedra pulled the mask of flames onto herself, and the body of her double flared into a blazing torch.

The Theena Shee retreated before the immolated woman. Sparks flew, the cottage kindled, and the thatched roof blasted into a conflagration that painted the night red.

2.
LOVE CUT WITH FEAR

Love is a memory of wings.
—Sappho

Standing among the trees, Flannery and Chet stared nervously at the holocaust and the Theena Shee scattering in confusion.

"Your grandmother is a kick in the head," Chet mumbled, watching the fumes of her wicked-out body—or ectoplasmic double or whatever that was—ribbon straight upward and linger against the night like a gigantic phantom stick of licorice.

"Let's get out of here before they come after us." Flannery tugged on the shreds of his sleeve.

"Which way?" He pivoted on his heels and surveyed in every direction rolling miles of lightless, uninhabited forest. "I think we're more likely to find a lost Boy Scout troop out there than a city."

"Let's just go." Flannery headed down a forest avenue speckled with moonlight. "We'll keep moving away from where we came."

"You heard what Nedra said." Chet caught her by the elbow. "The Theena Shee are tracking my scent. We won't get far if we stay together."

"We're not splitting up." She held his anxious stare with the composure of a professional assassin. "We're getting out together."

"Why?" His puzzled eyes searched her elfin, half-human face obstinately. "Why do you care about me?"

"It's the right thing to do," she answered curtly and turned back to the owlish dark. "Let's go."

"Is that it?" He took giant strides and came around in front of her. "Is that what this is all about? The right thing? Is that why I came after you and

129

got thrown into hell? Is that why you came after me?" He swung his jaw to one side, a feverish sheen in his handsome eyes, as if he were striving to visualize the shape of her soul. "Are we just here because we're doing the right thing?"

"If you keep yakking," she admonished with a displeased pout, "you'll be telling it to the dragon."

"That's why we should split up," he said with pragmatic certitude. "It's not about doing the right thing. It's about survival. Now, you go . . . "

Flannery clasped Chet's face in her hands and kissed him fiercely. He stared, eyes agog, but didn't resist as she pressed against him, her strength surprising. She broke the kiss and regarded him with soft ardor. Then, she reached out and lightly touched his lips. "I've never kissed anyone before."

After a spacious moment, Chet figured, "It's the glamour."

"Yeah—the glamour." Flannery took his hand. "We better get going." She closed one eye skeptically. "Are you coming with me—or do you still want to split up?"

Chet squeezed her hand. "Let's get out of here."

They stepped into darkness blue with moonlight, and she pointed through the trees to a final glimpse of the cottage burning and crackling. The Theena Shee had spread out across the clearing and were entering the woods individually at widely-spaced intervals.

"They're not coming after us in a pack," Chet said, showing the whites of his eyes. "They're stalking us separately, like hunters."

"The smoke has masked your scent." She drew him after her into a stand of sinewy pines. "They've lost us for now. Come on."

Among lunar threads and moonbeams, they hurried into the woods.

"I got an idea." His words wobbled with the jarring pace of their flight. "We can look for a brook and stay in the water, follow it out."

"The Theena Shee will find us and stone us." She veered toward a hedge—a wall of hawthorn—shimmering with moonlight. "I have a better idea."

They squeezed among the close-packed stilts of hawthorn branches, prying them aside to reach the hollow of mossy ground within.

In the braided moonlight of that narrow space, Flannery told him, "Take off your clothes."

A heavy breath of doubt blew through him. "What good will that do?"

"There's no time to explain." Gripped with trepidation, she peeked out the bars of the hedge. "We have to act while they're still looking for us separately." She met his unhappy frown calmly. "Trust me."

"But I'm not wearing any underwear."

"Go in there, behind the hedge, and take off your clothes." She shoved him through a gap in the clumped branches. "Give them to me. Hurry."

"Your grandmother made me do this, too." Chet's frown thickened, and he pressed through to the far side of the hedge where moonlight stood like glass rods between the crowded trees. "What is it with witches and nudity?"

"You think I'm a witch?" she asked with a tone of voice close to heartbreak.

"I thought maybe it might be a family tradition." He thrust his ragged shirt and torn jeans into the hawthorn brake. "Here."

"I'm not a witch." Flannery draped the shredded garments over the branches of the hedge and stuffed the sleeves and legs with dried leaves. Then, she bunched together leafy hawthorn twigs atop the shirt to resemble a head. "You have to be human to be a witch."

"What?"

"You heard me." She wedged herself through the gap to where Chet stood naked in the moonlight. "Yesterday, Nedra told me my mother was Theena Shee."

He crossed his hands in front of himself like a soccer player protecting the goal. "You're only half human?"

"Does that weird you out?" She lifted her jaw, defying him to tell her the truth. "I mean, it does weird you out, doesn't it?"

Chet winced a smile. "Standing naked in front of you in a spooky parallel world at night while beast-people stalk us for a sacrifice to their dragon—*that* weirds me out."

"After all that's happened, you can still joke?"

"Who's joking?"

Flannery began to smile, then raised a silencing finger to her mouth. "Listen!"

Distantly, a doleful piper blew a solitary air.

"Lie down!" Flannery pressed the femur wand across his chest and gruffly coaxed him to lie back. He dropped to his back atop the mossy ground, and she draped herself over him. Her hand covered his mouth, stifling his protest. "If I blanket you with my gown, they can't smell you." She tented him in her long hair, her face close to his. Slowly, she removed her hand from his mouth.

"Now I'm sure I'm dreaming," he whispered. "But in my dreams, you're the one that's naked."

"Stay still." Her breath tickled his ear and inspired goosebumps across his nakedness. "One of them is coming."

Only abject fear of the imps getting hold of him again kept his desire and all intimations of arousal in check. "And how is lying here like this going to help us?"

"You'll see." Her voice dropped an octave. "Are you scared?"

"I'm too scared to be scared."

"Maybe we should think about something else."

"How about the spring dance?" Chet asked helpfully. "I'm not much of a dancer. The fox trot and ants in my pants are the only two moves I really know."

"You still want to go to the dance with me?" she asked, her voice broken with worry. "I mean, now that you know what I am?"

"I'm naked. What are you?"

"Don't joke, Chet," she said, with an undercurrent of annoyance. "I just found out I'm a genuine freak."

"Sure—" he reacted as gently as he could manage, given the terror cramping his heart. "Now you have a cool excuse for not being liked. Me— I'm just not liked. I've got no excuse."

"At least you're human."

"For what that's worth." He locked his attention on the astonishing green of her eyes and tried not to think doomful thoughts about the enclosing night. "I'm just another conspicuous consumer among the billions. But you're different. Your chromosomes must be amazing."

"Thanks, Chet." She let out a soft, hopeless sigh. "That makes me feel a whole lot better."

"No, I mean it." He dared bring his hands up and cup her face. "You're unique. You're not like anyone else. That's why I fell in love with you."

Her eyebrows pinched together. "What do you know about love?"

"I'd like to find out with you."

The wistful piping intensified, leaves rustled and twigs snapped.

"One of them is coming!" Flannery expressed this obviously frightful fact so eagerly, almost happily, that Chet squirmed trying to contain the extremes of despair and hope she inspired. "Stop squirming!"

Beast eyes gleamed in the forest gloom—and into the moonlight stepped a robust Theena Shee with brush-cut hair and face like a ferret. Orange eyes flexed aggressively, catching sight of the man-shape cowering within the hawthorn. The scent of prey filled the hunter with blood-frenzy, and he attacked with a rampageous shout, hands clawing into the hedge and ripping out—a scarecrow.

The ferret face gawked with perplexity at the torn fabric in his hands. The instant that understanding congealed across his brute features, Flannery popped through the hedge, grinning wickedly. Her wand cracked the Theena Shee between his feral eyes, and he slumped in a senseless heap.

Chet wriggled out of the hedge and found Flannery crouched over the unconscious figure, stripping him. As the items of clothing came off the Theena Shee, he donned them. Moments later, he posed for her in fawnskin pants, tasseled kid leather shoes, and chemise stitched with Celtic knots. "How do I look?"

"Great—" she replied, not even looking, her attention already running through the shining forest. "And you smell even better. They'll never track us now."

3.
WHAT IS WHAT WE CANNOT SAY IS

The Daoine Sidhe are famous hunters, who befuddle their quarry with hedges of mist and rolling combers of fog.
—Joseph Goreu, *The Old Religion*

Arden marched angrily through white hot moonlight, eyes fiery red. A surly gang of Theena Shee followed. "Flannery!" he shouted into the night. "Where do you think you're running? You're in the Otherworld. There is no way out. Bring the boy to me. He is not one of us. Give him up—and you will live."

Behind him, his cohorts muttered angrily: "His scent is gone."—"It's the half-breed! She masks him with power she draws from the moon."—"She has no power. She's dirty blood."

Arden silenced them with an irate chop of his hand. "If we cannot find them, then we must make sure they cannot find themselves." He passed a dangerous look to the others. "Summon the dragon."

He spun to a blur, and the others did the same, emitting a whistle abrasive as ice wind in a dead tree's boughs.

The moony night's tendrils of mist thickened to fog—and the fog roiled like white water over the bumpy roots, climbing higher up the twisted trunks, inundating the forest in a blinding rush of white void.

4.

BREAKDOWN AT THE BRINK

Along the shore of the sky, at the brink of stars,
the cliffside of mystery overpeers infinity.
—**Aleister Crowley,** *Liber 777*

A dense fog phosphorescent with moonlight enclosed Flannery and Chet. They staggered and stumbled about, arms locked against the moan of a netherworld wind that ululated weirdly around them.

"I don't see any city lights," Chet complained, his voice creased with fear. "I don't see anything at all! Where are we?"

"We're lost." Flannery drew him closer and felt ahead with the elk thigh-bone. "We have to listen for Nedra. She'll call for us."

"All I hear is wind." His features, charged with fright, shivered, each with its own vibration: Eyes jittering, lips quivering, nostrils twitching like a rabbit's, his face looked ready to explode. He struggled to sound calm, and still his words crashed out of him, "We should stay where we are!"

"They'll find us." She leaned forward, taking long strides, urging him to hurry. "We've got to keep moving before they . . . "

With a jarred cry, Flannery fell, yanking Chet to his knees. He yelped painfully, shoulder socket electrified, her full weight tugging at him as she swung below, legs kicking in a void.

The fog ripped open, slashed apart by a sudden screaming gust that exposed Flannery dangling above a sheer plummet. Moonlit vapors and a river of fog streamed through a craggy precipice far below. Swinging rampantly, gripped only by Chet's straining arm, she dropped the wand. It toppled sedately into imponderable depths.

"Chet!" The storm wind sharpened to a banshee shriek and swept her shout away. "I dropped the wand!"

"Forget the wand!" Chet's operatic cry carried the searing pain of his arm out into the night. "Forget it!"

"I'm doomed without it!" She locked her horrified gaze on his. Something altered in her face, and her hand relaxed on his wrist, almost ripping his arm from its socket. "Let me go! Save yourself."

Chet's clenched eyes pried open, lit with tears, face shining with pain. "Don't you let go!" His command lashed out so forcefully, her fingers tightened again on his wrist. "Haven't you got it yet?" He hammered each word with a grunt, pressing his entire frame flat onto the earth, gaining purchase with his one free arm, legs spread and shoes dug in. "I'm never letting you go."

He pulled through his agony, enough for her to reach out with her flailing arm and both legs and latch onto the rooty brim of the cliff. Buoyant ease suffused his body immediately, Flannery's weight shared now with the face of rock. She scrabbled up over the edge and collapsed at his side, hissing sharp breaths of exertion and terror.

Before they could congratulate each other, the whistling wind stopped all at once, and a stillness of shimmering silence enclosed the cliff edge like an enchantment. Footfalls approached slow and easy—and, out of the fog, Arden strolled, twirling the femur wand. His smile mocked her. Without dark glasses, his vague eyebrows and deep sockets lent his face the honed contours of a skull.

Fog rolled back, unveiling around him his brutish gang of Theena Shee, with their chopped hair and scowling faces perforated with sterling posts, clasps, and razor wire—and, behind them, visible through a scrim of skinny trees, the glittering city skyline.

Arden pointed the bulbous end of the thighbone at the couple huddled among the tall grass and looping roots at the cliff's edge. "Word to your tailor, Chester."

"Leave him alone, Arden." Her tone, intended to sound defiant, came out in a frightened, whinnying breath.

The prince of the Otherworld swung the femur at the distant shining skyscrapers. "Escape was closer than you realized." Then, he aimed the wand over the cliff at indigo depths of rocky ledges and cliff walls angling far below to a molten vein of lava. "Death closer yet."

Rising up from that churning river of magma, a viperous shape slithered. It could have been sulfur fumes—until they heard it bellow, a subway rumble, a jet engine roar.

Flannery and Chet scrambled to their feet and edged away from the cliff.

"Destroying my bike in the pit was a malicious act, Flannery." Arden closed in, followed by his thugs. "Now, I've not only lost a good set of wheels and a tough old tree, you've disturbed the dragon—and it must be fed."

"You lied to me," said Flannery, jut-jawed. "You said your victims died swiftly. I saw the dragon grotto, Arden,"

"A white lie." His reply, thickly layered with rage, bitterness, and sadistic glee swung at her like a club. "I didn't want to alarm you with grisly details. Truth is, we have to keep reserves. Who knows when the dragon will be hungry?"

"You lied." Her tone, sickly with hurt, fended his wrathful attack. "You said you loved me."

"Love?" He tilted his head to one side as if trying to remember. "No. I never breathed that word. I said I wanted you. I still do, Flannery. I showed you a good time. We had fun. If I truly hated mixed breeds, I would have thrown you into the dragon pit immediately—the way the others did your parents."

This news struck Flannery hard, and she sobbed, "You killed my mother and father?"

"The others did that." He closed in, speaking softer, as if imparting a confidence. "I had nothing to do with it. I think mixed breeds have a hybrid vigor that is exciting. That's why I wanted to keep you for myself. I could still make you one of us."

The muscles of Flannery's face hardened. "I will never be one of you."

"Then, dragon food." Arden shrugged, voice little more than a whisper.

Flannery reached for Chet, who cowered behind her, and pulled him close, her mouth touching his ear. "If you really care about me," she imparted, breathless and faint, "save yourself. Get out of here—*now!*"

137

Shouting that last word, she pushed him away. He staggered back, blast-ed both by the paralyzing beauty of her abrupt anger—and the mobilizing fright of confronting the tiger yellow of her bestial eyes.

Howling, she lunged at Arden. She moved with uncanny speed—a smear of motion. She and the faerïe prince collided in a tangle of limbs reminiscent to Chet of their former passionate dancing. For an eyeblink, they danced fiercely together in the tall grass, and then they veered over the lip of the cliff and dropped away.

5.
KILLING WITH THE EDGE OF THE MOON

The infinite Abyss 'tis a void boundless as a nether sky.
—William Blake, *The Marriage of Heaven and Hell*

Locked in vehement embrace—his hands at her throat, her fingers clawing his face, legs hacking huge, wild kicks—Arden and Flannery toppled into a gulf of emptiness. The femur wand spun through the air with them, catching moonlight like a platinum pinwheel.

Wailing, the Theena Shee rushed to the brink and stood there tottering, mewling in fright and despair. Then, stunned silence gripped them as they watched the struggling couple dwindle among swirling mists. Arden's furious cry pierced the thunder from the rising dragon, and the anguished Theena Shee bawled again as one.

Chet backed away from the distracted Theena Shee. Horror at Flannery's barbarous act whirled him about, and he ran toward the bright city beyond the trees. Far back in the woods, headlights from a highway twinkled.

The mounting blare of the aroused dragon resonated forcefully, a rocket engine that flogged Chet faster. In the din, he heard the chambers of his heart ringing, resounding with the memory of Flannery's promise, *We're not splitting up. We're getting out together.*

Chet jogged to a stop. The haunting recollection of her voice played off depths of desire that he had been excavating for too long alone. The anguish on his face fell away, replaced by a placid expression of determination. "We're not splitting up."

He turned and stared past the lunar lit trees to where the Theena Shee milled in confusion. Uttering a bitter sob, he spurred himself into a mad dash back the way he had come.

The Theena Shee, hearing his frantic approach, faced about, hissing with astonishment at his attack. They reached out to catch him, but he had thrown all his strength into his run. Flannery was gone now, plummeting away like a dream, leaving him only the nightmare remnants of exile in the Otherworld—or, worse, return to an ordinary existence, college, career, a conventional life eventually surrendering to withering old age and remorseful recollections of a magical love that never was.

No!

The orange-eyed creatures in their hostile human masks would not stop him. He thrust them aside with tantrum fury and bowled over those in his way. Hurling a triumphant shout ahead, he flung himself over the brink, arms outstretched, hugging all of space.

6.
FURIOUS ANGELS

Love and desire are the heart's furious angels.
—Welsh saying

In freefall, arms and legs spread—a human star—Chet dove through wisps of neon mist. He grimaced against the assault of dragon noise and heat that streaked back his hair and pressed his elfin garments against him fluttering and snapping. The thermal updraft drizzled with radiant sparks, slowing his plunge.

Out of the haze, a rocky slope slewed toward him, and he pulled up his legs at the last moment and landed with a grunt. The momentum of his impact sent him skidding and tumbling down the incline in a rattle of pebbles and gravel. He came to rest on a rock shelf gleaming wetly in the moonlight, head and shoulders thrust over the void.

Miles below, he sighted the dragon ascending, a whiplash of fire with jaws of tarry smoke and blue-white fangs hot as lightning. Its enraged squall shook the cliffs, knocking loose boulders and sizzling streams of debris.

Chet shinnied back from the edge gasping. He stood and nearly slipped on the wet rocks. Trickling water flowed from a large, ribbed and rusty pipe, huge as a cave, protruding from the cliff wall. He identified it as one of the city's drainage ducts, seeping gutter runoff. It existed here in the Otherworld, he knew, by magic, evoked by his deep desire to escape—just like this ledge that had miraculously materialized to break his fall.

Gagging, gargled sounds snagged his attention. He slogged upslope over slippery pebbles that slid his kid leather shoes out from under, impeding his progress and obliging him to crouch and brace himself with his hands, advancing like an ape. Atop the bank of slick stones, he staggered to a stop.

Arden and Flannery, illuminated by moonlight and the stuttering red flares of swirling dragon sparks, lay on a disintegrating ledge locked in combat. Arden squatted over her, the femur wand pressed against her throat, strangling her as she futilely kicked and bucked.

From above, the Theena Shee came sliding down the moonlit gravel slopes, hooting and shrieking. In the argent light, their churlish features looked less like faces than masks, gouged eyeholes carnivorously alert, mouths wide gashes of ravening teeth.

Grabbing a fist-sized rock, Chet scuttled along the stony ledge. He approached from behind Arden, who had writhing Flannery pinned under him. The dragon's bellowing muted the clatter of Chet's sliding advance over the loose stones. He raised his arm to strike, and Arden spun about, swinging the thighbone.

The heavy wand knocked the rock from Chet's grasp, and he reeled backward, sliding over the raspy gravel, careening right to the edge of the cliff. There, he teetered, arms waving, against a torrent of sparks that plumed upward with the tempest howl of the dragon.

The Theena Shee skidded onto the ledge, snickering and leering at Chet. Barking a laugh at the arrival of his comrades, Arden rose from limp Flannery.

"Looks like you were right after all, Chester." The prince of the Theena Shee heel-stepped down the flinty bank toward Chet, animal eyes flashing in the glare of rushing sparks. "I am the Devil!" He touched Chet's heart with the knobbed end of the wand. "And I'm sending you straight to hell." Smilingly coldly, he nudged Chet off the cliff.

Chet dropped from sight, and the Theena Shee bleated laughter and danced with mirthful, pelvic abandon on the cliff rim. Eleven heartbeats later, while the frenzied dancers were in the midst of 'shaking their tail feathers,' 'riding their ponies,' and 'walking like Egyptians,' a gale of whipped sparks heaved Chet back onto the ledge. He collided with a startled Arden, knocking him to the ground.

"Can't go to hell," Chet gasped, breath blowing loud as a horse's, face shining with terror. "Hell's coming to us!"

Behind him, the huge and terrible head of the dragon reared up with a behemoth roar. The cyclone brunt of the blast tossed the Theena Shee about like dolls and lifted Flannery, dashing her against the cliff wall and slamming her alert. Sparks flared everywhere like infuriated hornets.

Commanding furious strength, Arden stood, hoisting Chet into the spark-spinning air with one hand and with the other raising the femur wand to brain him. "Lord of the Abyss!" he shouted to the apparition of flaming vapors and clotted smoke, the dragon big as sunset. "Take this human sacrifice and be fulfilled! Eater of Souls! Devour this man and be pleased with your servants, the Theena Shee!"

Stunned and staring, Chet hung limp. But before the weapon could strike, Flannery seized the femur wand from behind. She jerked Arden around, facing him with eyes human once more and tight with scorn.

"Eat this!" Her left hook cracked him under the jaw, and he dropped Chet and lurched backward, eyes rolling.

Wand in hand, Flannery grabbed Chet and boosted him upright. The dragon loomed over them, a firecloud gorgon, cleft brows veined with voltage and horned with bituminous twists of slag. Malformed jaws widened, drooling fumes, exhaling a storm of sparks through which molten eyes scanned for prey.

7.
HELLHOLE

. . . nor can the swift outrun death.
—*Wisdom Is a Butterfly* (Irish ballad)

Arden rocked upright, rubbing his jaw, and ordered in a smeared voice, "Take them!"

The Theena Shee hustled across broken ground through dazzling motes of fire under the baleful visage of the dragon. They clambered up a gravel slope and down the other side, descending on Flannery and Chet.

Flannery wielded the femur wand, prepared to fight.

"The drain pipe from the city!" Chet shouted against the squalling dragon. "The water will stop them!"

They scurried through smog exhaled by the giant fire lizard, a filthy haze that burned eyes and skin at the same time that it obscured their flight. The dragon's fire-swollen head swung above, vainly trying to fix this moving target in a chaos of surging smoke and gyrating sparks.

The clawing hands of the Theena Shee snatched emptiness as Flannery and Chet sprang into the cavernous opening of the drainage duct. Water sloshed around their ankles, and the frustrated yelps of the Theena Shee reverberated in the dark conduit.

The fleeing couple stopped and turned to see, encircled within the giant mouth of the corroded pipe, Arden and the Theena Shee dwarfed by the malignant and fiery immensity of the dragon's head—a cankerous paisley of blue sparks crawling over a bulbous and horned brow—a huge cliff over-hanging venomous eyes.

The faerïe prince shouted through the maelstrom of rushing sparks and fumes. What he yelled vanished in the imbecile din. He writhed a fury dance in the knelling glare of dragon fire, and his gang stomped their thwarted hostility.

Flannery stood legs apart, femur wand upheld in jubilant outrage.

Chet, who had already run ahead, splashed back and grabbed her arm. "Come on! Let's go!"

"I despise you—all you murderers!" The glint of lunacy in her green eyes flexed, and Chet cringed, expecting her irises to blow out and congeal again to vicious puma orbs. "I'm not one of you. I'm a human being! And I'd rather be dead than like you!"

Arden and his malefic Theena Shee shook with so much rage they blurred to demonic vibrations. Their smudged shapes hardened to goblin marionettes, squalid trolls with enormously bloated heads and eelish tongues worming out contorted mouth holes.

Behind them, the dragon's serpent jaws unhinged, and a vortex of flames engulfed the trollish Theena Shee, dissolving them to sparkling ash, and filling the drainage duct with their anguished screams and a swelling firecloud.

Chet pulled Flannery's arm, and they sped deeper into the pipe, fleeing the roiling inferno. Driven ahead of that turbulent fireball, webs of soot tangled, meshed, and wove tightly into the writhing, snarling shadow of the black dog.

Ice eyes glaring, fur like black quills, the massive mongrel lunged through the drainage duct leaving behind the dragon's blaze that had created her. Bizarrely, blue flames seethed through her fangs, and her malign barks stretched to a hellish blort of brutal noise.

Flannery and Chet raced deeper into the unlit tunnel, the monster at their heels. Swinging around with the wand gripped like a cudgel, Flannery rapped the slavering snout and sent the beast careening into the dark.

The diabolic thing thrashed violently in the shallow drain water before bouncing back, eyes popping with manic furor and fang-filled jaws flaring unnaturally wide. Her victims, whipped with fright, sprang ahead. Flares from the fire-huffing creature illuminated their delirious flight in crimson, torn silhouettes.

At a fork in the drainage channels, they splashed to a stop, clutching at each other. Echoes of the pursuing death-demon overlapped in a horrible cavalcade of ripping snarls and distorted yawps.

"Which way?" Chet's fear blazed, coming in short, breathless heaves as his hands slapped the slimy wall that split the conduit left and right.

Flannery leaned on him, hissing for air, "Listen—"

From the left came a distant call, barely audible above the eerie, rippling yowls of the death-dog—"Flower Face . . . "

"This way!" Flannery pushed him into the leftward darkness as the black dog veered toward them, flames drooling in fiery slobber from her raving jaws.

8.
THE FETCH

Only the high of heart can hear love's whispered
promise above the outspoken grave.
—Dr. Rhodius Evans, *Folklore of the Bards*

"Flower Face—hurry!" Nedra's call arrived clutched with echoes. "Up here!"

A vertical shaft of moonlight glowed like a chrome trunk at the far end of the duct. The rabid clamor of the black dog intensified, racing with Flannery and Chet to the pillar of moonlight and an iron ladder set in the stone wall.

"Go!" Flannery demanded, pushing Chet ahead. She stood her ground, swinging the sturdy bone energetically at the charging monstrosity. "Get up the ladder! I'm right behind you."

Chet stopped so short he doubled over, arms windmilling. "Flannery!" He hastened back to where she crouched with the femur wand in a double-handed grip, ready to do battle with the hulk of electrified black fur and wrinkled muzzle of unsheathed, flesh-ripping teeth. "Not a good idea." He locked his arms around her waist and hauled her away just as the abomination snorted twin jets of blue fire.

Flannery writhed free of Chet's hold and backhanded the thighbone, clubbing the lunging predator hard across the muzzle. The creature staggered to one side and shook her large head to an inky blur.

As startled as if she'd just slammed an ace in tennis, Flannery stood staring, registering her advantage, until Chet yelled, "Come on!"

They launched toward the pillar of moonlight while the dog refocused her hateful eyes and hurtled after them.

At the metal rungs in the stone wall, the desperate couple looked up to see Nedra's rumpled face and halo of silver hair backlit by the moon. She smiled delightedly as if she'd just stumbled upon them in hide-and-seek. "There you are!"

"Climb!" Flannery rammed Chet with her back and batted at the narrowing space between them and the grotesque shadowshape. "Go! Go!"

Chet scooted up the rungs. At the top, the witch's strong arms hooked him under his shoulders and lifted him into the night air. He sat on the rim of a manhole and stared down between his knees at Flannery's red hair flailing like flames as she fended off the beast. Her name jammed in his throat with a sob of terror.

The witch shoved him back and stuck her head in the hole. "Get up here, Flower Face!"

Flannery met the ice-fire eyes of the shouting dog with cold recognition. This was her death. Her unhappiness with life had summoned this ripper. That was why Nedra had worked her dark ceremony in the first place, to help the forlorn girl. Now that Flannery understood why she had always felt so detached—now that she knew she was only half human—she realized the black dog was not a foe.

If she wanted her to, the bitch would cut through Flannery's heartache with claws and set her free.

To her surprise, the thought of dying no longer seemed an option. She had returned to the Otherworld ready to exchange her life for Chet's—not because she cared for him but because she had no real care for her own disconnected life. But now—she bashed the femur wand hard at the loud harrier, driving her back—it felt like the green moment before lightning strikes. A long gloom had climaxed. She wanted to live.

She leaped onto the ladder, grasping a rung with one hand while slashing the femur wand at the abhorrent jaws grinding and snapping at her heels. Slowly, she mounted the ladder. The mauler leaped, biting for her legs, and she smacked the furious canine squarely on the skull. The brute fell back shrieking, all the more wrathful.

From the moon-gleaming water, the black dog rose, stretching to a phantasmagorical humanoid with ripping claws and a shark-shriek mouth of stabbing red teeth. Flannery threw the wand upward and reached for the top rungs with a despairing cry.

Chet and Nedra each took hold of an arm and hauled her into the cool night. She rose through the manhole onto the asphalt and collapsed dumbfounded with recognition at the exact spot where the school bus had struck her.

That stunning recollection passed in a single flutter of her terrified heart, and she quickly muscled the manhole cover back into place. It clanged shut—then, clanged again and wobbled, struck hard from below.

Across the parking lot, a slow traffic of limousines, taxis, and cars discharged students in party clothes. Only a few stared incredulously across the dark lot at the two beautiful kids who had crawled up from underground. Most of the couples gave their cheerful attention to the festively illuminated high school sprawling beneath the voluptuous moon.

Dance music spilled from the gymnasium's open doors, which framed a postcard-shaped glimpse back in time to a dance of a more innocent age: A gaiety of streamers and balloons decorated the rafters around a glitter ball flashing laser rays over a crowd of bopping students in casual-hip party attire.

"You both smell like roses!" Nedra laughed and helped Chet steady Flannery. "I've never seen such strong glamour come out of a sewer! Bless my eyes—look at the two of you. Such a lovely couple."

Welded together with looks of terror, Chet and Flannery seized Nedra by either arm. "The black dog!" Flannery wept.

"She's *Death!*" Chet added loudly, ears still numb from the blaring of the dragon. "And she's right behind us!"

"Hush, children—hush." Nedra mildly shrugged off their grasping hands. "Leave the black dog to me."

"No, Neddie!" Flannery's words toppled out, rattling with fear. She yanked the thighbone from Chet's hand and waved it defensively at the manhole. "The Theena Shee gave her dragon force! She'll kill you!"

The manhole clanged again, spurting blue flames.

Chet took the two women by their elbows and tried to guide them away from the gonging manhole. "Let's scram!"

"Tsk, Chester." Nedra tugged her arm free and gently and sadly rebuked him. "You should know by now, you can't run from the black dog. We must give her what she wants."

"Neddie, please." Flannery searched the old woman's peaceful face, hoping to find some of the crone's former mettle. Instead, she saw only the witch's tranquility and tired eyes, eyes hooded with resignation. "Don't do this. There must be some magic we can work."

"Flower Face, you have worked all the magic you need to work." Nedra removed the femur wand from Flannery's hands. "You've brought this wand back from the cave of the dragon. Now, you are safe forever from the Theena Shee." She tenderly caressed Flannery's cheek. "I summoned the black dog. I will meet her." She assumed a wide stance over the juddering manhole.

Flannery embraced her grandmother and sobbed, "Neddie!"

"I'm old, Flannery." Nedra sounded irritated as she shouldered the young woman aside. "I know what I'm doing." She stooped, then glanced sideways, aiming a kindly smile at the teenager. "I *am* glad to see you care about this old woman. You've found your heart, Flower Face. I don't have to worry about you anymore."

With a vigorous grunt, Nedra budged aside the manhole, and it rasped across the asphalt. A vibrant howl shook the night—and the black dog flowed forth slick and glossy as an oil spill. Out of that ooze, she jumped up on all fours, a big-shouldered canine, a ravager growling with malice.

Flannery moved to protect Nedra, but Chet threw his arms around her and pulled her back. He tried to utter something meaningful like, "She's a Wiccan priestess—she knows what she's doing—" But he could barely breathe let alone speak above the booming of his heart. Relief poured through him to see the hideous monster glowering at the witch and not them.

"Neddie!" Flannery hitched in Chet's embrace, but he would not release her.

With unexpected speed, Nedra sprinted away from them, across the parking lot, rope sandals slapping sharply on the tarmac, sounding explosively like a string of firecrackers. A few couples still drifting toward the gym paused and glanced at the swift old woman swinging the big elk bone over her gray head and chortling with giddy abandon. The black dog chased her, snarling and barking harshly, blue sparks spinning off her bristling fur.

At the empty, far end of the lot, beyond the last puddles of orange light from the lampposts, the witch hurled the wand into the sky. It spun end-over-end, shining in the moonlight, climbing higher and higher, impossibly high. And the black dog leaped after it, pouncing over Nedra's head and into the night.

The beast's amok barks dimmed as she rushed across the face of the moon. Pursuing the last glinting twinkle of the femur wand among the stars, her hulking, shadow-black body disappeared.

Flannery and Chet, his arms still tightly around her, gazed open-mouthed with astonishment as Nedra moseyed back to them, dusting off her hands. The dance couples who had paused searched the sky with wondering, disbelieving expressions and shook their heads at the old woman, not sure what they had just witnessed.

"Dogs love to fetch a good bone," the witch explained loudly and with a hearty laugh, and then whispered victoriously to herself, "Well now, old girl, that should be good for at least seven more years."

9.
DREAMS PASS LIKE STARLIGHT

*In the days when Mab was queen and the
world knew much of magic . . .*

Nedra put thumb and index finger to her crinkled mouth and whistled crisply. A taxi in front of the gym responded, its backup lights brightening as it reversed along the curb. "I'm going home," the old woman announced with a fatigued smile. "And you two are going to the dance."

Chet and Flannery shared a look of wonder, still held together by his encircling arms.

"Why the surprise?" the witch asked through her crooked smile. "Any manhole in the city is as close to the Otherworld as this one. I brought you out here so you could celebrate." She winked. "All's well that escapes hell! Eh?"

"It's not coming back?" Flannery asked anxiously.

"The black dog always comes back." Nedra lifted a bitter stare to the frail stars, then crimped a smile with her thin lips. "But not anytime soon."

Flannery and Chet, arms around each other, stood wordlessly as the taxi backed up to where the witch waited. They might as well have been rooted to the ocean floor watching starfish browse, they appeared that breathless and amazed.

"You're both beautiful." Nedra opened the taxi door. "You wear your glamour well. Enjoy it. You earned it." She got in, closed the door and rolled down the window. "I'll call your parents and tell them you're alive." Her polar blue eyes surveyed Chet seriously. "The explanations I'll leave to you, young man. Just come up with a good story—and don't dare think of telling them the truth. No one will believe you." She wiggled her thick fingers. "Ta, children."

The taxi pulled away, and the witch's hoary head popped out the window. "Chester—you get her back by dawn!"

Flannery and Chet watched the taxi roll across the parking lot and merge into the flow of traffic. Their terrified embrace relaxed, and they faced each other, astounded and beginning to shiver.

Printed in the United States
61888LVS00007B/33

9 780809 556977